DEATH VISITS
KEMPSHOTT HOUSE

Nick Shaw, travel writer and enthusiastic archer, expects to spend an enjoyable weekend with his partner, Louisa, at the luxurious Kempshott House Hotel. Then a body is discovered during an archery club contest on the hotel's grounds, stuck through with three arrows. The police are called in, assisted by Louisa — a detective sergeant — and it soon becomes apparent that the man has been deliberately murdered. Worse still, it would appear that the murderer hasn't finished yet . . .

KATHERINE HUTTON

DEATH VISITS KEMPSHOTT HOUSE

Complete and Unabridged

LINFORD
Leicester

First published in Great Britain

First Linford Edition
published 2015

A catalogue record for this book is available
from the British Library.

ISBN 978–1–4448–2447–6

Published by
F. A. Thorpe (Publishing)
Anstey, Leicestershire

Set by Words & Graphics Ltd.
Anstey, Leicestershire
Printed and bound in Great Britain by
T. J. International Ltd., Padstow, Cornwall

This book is printed on acid-free paper

1

Kempshott House Hotel was originally built in the 1790s for the Perceval family and period features abound in the seventeen guest rooms. Falconry, archery and clay pigeon shooting can be enjoyed on arrangement with the front desk. For the even more adventurous, it has been known for a corpse to be discovered in the extensive grounds of the hotel.

'Oh, God. I'm never going to be able to write this!' Nick Shaw groaned as he screwed up another piece of paper and pitched it towards the bin.

'Do you have to get it done quite yet?' Louisa West asked as she retrieved the sheet, read it, grimaced and consigned it once more to oblivion.

'I always like to get the bones of a write-up done while I'm still on site, in case I have more questions for the hoteliers. It saves time later.' Shaw sighed. 'Though this time I think I'll have to get a bit of distance to be able to do it justice. It's not the hotel's fault that they've had a murder here.'

★   ★   ★

The weekend had begun so promisingly . . .

The long, sweeping driveway curved slightly so that Kempshott House was not visible from the road. As he rounded the bend, Shaw was greeted by the imposing sight of a large classical building, not exactly pretty, but certainly impressive. From the hotel's brochure he knew it had been built in the late eighteenth century and modified at various times to suit the taste of successive occupants. It looked solid and welcoming. His heart rose at the sight of it and the thought of a much-needed drink. It had taken him an hour longer than he had anticipated to reach the hotel; the Friday traffic had been bad and he had taken a few wrong turns as usual. For someone who travelled for a living he had a lousy sense of direction.

Following the signs to the car park,

Shaw pulled to a stop and turned off the engine with a sigh of relief. The late-afternoon sunlight on that April day had been in his eyes for most of the journey, making it even harder to read the road signs. If Louisa had been able to come with him he knew they would have been here long before now, but she was hoping to join him on the Saturday morning in time to register as a latecomer for the archery tournament. He had her kit in the car alongside his own, as she would be coming by train and it was pretty challenging to transport a six-foot longbow on public transport without getting in everyone's way.

Lifting his weekend bag out of the car, Shaw walked round to the front of the hotel, evaluating the building for his review and the grounds for their suitability as a field and target shoot arena. The wide lawn looked more likely to be a croquet lawn but he could see a marquee set up in a nearby field, close to a small wood. That must be the location of the tournament, he decided. Time enough to scout that out tomorrow. Tonight, he would concentrate on assessing the hotel itself. He was a travel correspondent for several newspapers and magazines and had built up a modest but dedicated following as a columnist. The fact that this assignment could be tackled in tandem with the chance to attend an archery contest was pure serendipity.

Kempshott House had agreed to host a weekend of shooting and to be honest, fairly serious drinking, on the usual understanding that the insurance was sorted out by the participants and in the hope that a decent number of archers would prefer to stay in the very pleasant surroundings of the hotel instead of paying the five-pound fee for pitching a tent or camper van in the field.

Shaw had breathed a sigh of relief at the thought of not having to struggle with his tent for once. It should be the perfect match of rugged, manly outdoor pursuit followed by sybaritic comfort.

'Another toxophilist I see! Welcome to Kempshott House.'

Shaw was greeted by a good-natured shout as he entered the lobby. A florid, fairly large man was approaching him with a broad smile on his face. He was taken aback for a moment as all his archery equipment was in the car; then he remembered he was wearing his shooting jacket which had a small pin in the shape of an archer on the lapel. Setting down his bag, he shook the proffered hand. 'You're very observant, to see the pin at once,' he said.

'Got to have an eye for detail in this business. Brendan Dering at your service, the owner of this beautiful place — every inch of oak panelling, every blade of grass. If anything is not absolutely perfect, you let me know.' The man had a slight southern Irish accent and a conspiratorial glint in his eye.

Shaw's heart sank. It seemed obvious that the owner had clocked more than his love of archery. It was always harder to do a fair review if the staff knew he was a travel writer. Still, he could always ask the other residents what their experience of the hotel was. Especially if they were also taking part in the weekend's events and he could talk away from the house.

'I'll let Stephanie look after you now, sir,' Dering said, scooping up his guest's bag and walking briskly to the expansive polished oak desk where a remarkably pretty woman was just ending a phone call. He nodded a greeting to Stephanie, who smiled and then turned her attention to Nick.

'Good afternoon, sir, and welcome to Kempshott House Hotel. Could I have your name please?'

'Nick Shaw. I have a booking for a double room as someone should be joining me tomorrow,' he replied, somehow omitting the word *girlfriend* from the sentence. The receptionist really was beautiful, with a wealth of soft curls around her shoulders and a green dress that was smart but nothing like a uniform. It was a pleasant change from the often severe corporate look many hotels insisted upon.

'Yes, I have your details here. A double room overlooking the garden for three nights.' She took the key from a row of hooks behind her. While Shaw filled in the usual forms she politely inquired: 'Are you here for the archery?'

'Indeed I am. I try to get to as many events like this as I can. I believe this is the first time your hotel has hosted one.'

'That's right, sir. Mr. Dering is keen to make full use of the grounds now that they're all part of the property. It took a while but he's very persistent.' The receptionist checked the forms and smiled. 'There are going to be visitors from all over Europe this weekend. It should be a good time.'

'If past events are anything to go by, it will be, particularly when the Dutch contingent arrive.' Shaw grinned and picked up his bag, heading for the grand staircase. As he rounded the corner of the stairs, he heard Dering's distinctive voice welcoming another guest with much the same patter as before. He brightened. If the hotel manager greeted everyone so ebulliently then maybe he hadn't recognised him as a travel writer after all. A few minutes later, surveying the view from his impressively luxurious room, he decided that this could be a very enjoyable weekend.

Drink in hand, Shaw wandered around the empty lounge examining the pictures on the walls, some of which showed Kempshott House at various stages of its development. As he was looking at a Victorian oil painting he heard an approaching group of guests and recognised a familiar voice. Smiling, he turned round. 'Hello, Smithy. Haven't seen you for a while.'

'Nick! Good to see you, mate.'

Shaw tried to avoid the bear hug but to no avail. At least his ribs felt intact this time.

Thick-set and barrel-chested, Jason 'Smithy' Bridges was one of a handful of archers who used a proper English warbow — a monstrous one-hundred-and-sixty-pound draw weight, seven-foot-long beast made from Italian high-altitude yew in the manner of the Mary Rose longbows. Although it was the envy of many who saw it, no one but he could string the bloody thing. A regular at archery meetings and a great devotee of traditional skills, he was a mechanic by training but had branched out into carpentry and metalwork, and he made his own arrows and archery-related accoutrements.

'Have you seen the course yet? It's a tricky bastard,' Smithy said happily. 'We've had a lot of fun setting it up.'

'Well, it's always good to know who to blame! Are you staying at the hotel?' Shaw asked, though he thought he knew the answer.

'God, no! I mean, it's the business and all that, but you can never really get properly drunk in a posh place, can you? I've got my tent pitched down at the campsite. Lovely field it is, with a bit behind a hedge for the portaloos.' Smithy steered his friend towards the bar. 'Let me give you a few tips about the course while you get the first round in.'

Shaw laughed and readily agreed. Drinking with Smithy was always an education one way or another.

It was about forty minutes later that they became aware of angry voices, slightly muffled but loud enough to catch the odd phrase.

'*I never would have allowed this.*

Disgusting rabble . . . no doubt in the morning you'll find all of the silverware has gone!'

'This is not the time, Margaret. Janice, why did you bring her tonight?'

Then a quieter voice Shaw couldn't make out.

Smithy had stopped talking too, to listen. 'Someone's none too pleased,' he commented thoughtfully. 'Do you think we're the *rabble*?'

'Speak for yourself; I'm perfectly respectable,' Shaw retorted good-naturedly. He looked around the now rather busy room, a motley gathering of archers who were keeping up a pleasant hum of convivial conversation. Looking through the doorway to the lobby of the hotel, he watched as Stephanie walked slowly to the door, supporting an elderly lady who he guessed may have been the source of the discontent. He wondered if she was a permanent resident.

'The car's here for you, Margaret. Janice can take you home. I'll let you know when we're having a quiet night and we can have a proper chat, like old

10

times,' said Stephanie.

'Thank you, my dear, I would like that,' the old lady replied, seemingly mollified.

'That girl's got a way with her,' Smithy exclaimed. 'I wonder what that was all about? I don't want the shoot causing any bad feelings among the locals.'

'It's not usually a problem, is it?' Shaw drained his glass and considered the advisability of stopping now to eat.

'Just occasionally. When we have to block off a footpath because it goes too close to the ranges, for instance, I've known ramblers to get a bit shirty, but most people are fine. We had one down at the practice butts earlier, a bearded guy who wanted to have a go with my bow.'

'Your bow! He wouldn't have a hope of pulling it,' Shaw said.

'That's pretty much what I told him and we had a chat about archery. He was all right, if a bit surprised that we were camping here all weekend.' Smithy rose to his feet. 'I'm going to love you and leave you for now. I want to have a word with one or two people before tomorrow.'

Shaw grinned. 'See you in the morning

11

then. I should get back to work anyway. Got to test out the dining facilities.'

'Back to the grindstone, eh? Bloody hell, it's a hard life!' Smithy laughed and headed for the bar.

Yes. It's a tough job but somebody's got to do it, Nick thought happily to himself as he strolled to the dining room.

★ ★ ★

Saturday morning was bright and crisp as the archers began to gather at the briefing area. Shaw had collected his bow, arrows, stand, finger tab and bracer from the car and followed the gravel path that led from the main grounds of the hotel to the fields that backed on to it. Greeting some old friends, he worked his way to a table that had been set up with registration forms and schedules. He signed in and quickly scanned the list to see if Louisa had arrived, but there was no sign as yet. He had left a message with the hotel staff — sadly not Stephanie this morning — that her archery kit was in their room, but it was possible that Louisa would register for the shoot first.

He wondered if this was going to be one of those times when she would turn up at the very last minute. It could be difficult for her to get away from work and he had lost count of the number of times he had given up on her, only to get a tap on the shoulder and a grin of welcome.

'Hello there, Nicholas!' came a booming, deeply accented voice.

Turning round, Shaw was greeted by the sight of a tall, robust, sandy-haired man dressed in authentic early medieval garb, right down to the leather thongs holding his leggings on. 'Lars! Good to see you,' he said, genuinely pleased. Lars was a Norwegian archer who often turned up on the circuit. 'How's the family — are they with you?'

'Yes. The kids are still in the RV. They're too tired after the journey but Karin should be here soon.'

Lars and Karin's RV was legendary. A beautiful monster of a thing. The big daddy of all camper vans. For a couple who took re-enactment quite seriously, they still chose comfort over verisimilitude when it came to camping.

A voice rang out over the general hubbub: 'Can all those participants who've already registered please move to the beer tent and let the others sign in? Use a bit of common sense, people!'

There was a bit of good-natured heckling of the announcer, a man Shaw had seen a couple of times before, but nevertheless a general shift towards the marquee started to happen. Inside, lists of teams were pinned up.

The morning's event was the field shoot — a misnomer if ever there was one, for it was held inside a small stretch of forest. Groups of no more than six would move round the woodland course, tackling the targets in turn and recording their scores. The targets were life-sized models of various animals and there were different points depending on where, if anywhere, the arrows hit. In effect it was an archery discipline which attempted to capture the thrill of actual hunting with a longbow, which was now illegal in Britain. Each team would go round twice with staggered starting times. After the initial bottleneck had cleared, it kept the momentum going nicely.

Shaw strolled round to examine the lists along with several others, most of whom he knew by sight, but there were a few obvious newcomers who were having the rules recapped for them by friends. A bearded man appeared to be on his own and wandered around, looking a little confused. Shaw would have gone over to talk to him but for the sudden feeling he had of being stalked. Turning round quickly, he saw Louisa already kitted up, ready to pounce.

'Oh, you noticed!' she complained. 'I wanted to surprise you.'

'You always do. I'm so glad you got here in time.' He hugged her and turned to indicate the lists. 'You and I are in the second group to go, about half an hour I'd guess until we can start.'

'Yes, there's a big crowd out there so I think most of us must be here.' Louisa adjusted the quiver around her waist and propped her bow against the wall of the tent. 'I like the hotel, by the way. Very swish. I hope you give it a good write-up.'

'Only time will tell, and I can't be bribed,' Shaw answered pompously, putting on a stern look.

'Has someone tried?' Louisa asked, suddenly serious.

'No, not really, more's the pity. How can I nobly resist temptation if no one bothers to tempt me?'

'Oh, you poor thing,' she mocked. 'Come on, we should stick near the organiser for announcements.'

'But he told us to come here before you turned up,' Shaw protested.

'He can't have. He walked down with me. It's Leon. You remember him?' Louisa contradicted him cheerfully.

True enough, when they emerged from the tent, Shaw saw the tall figure of Leon St. John keeping a watchful eye over the assembly. The man he had assumed to be in charge was now chatting to his companions. Although there was an acceptance that it was a good idea to have someone in charge of these events, and it certainly took some organising, many of the archers who gathered to compete were the chairmen or captains of their own local clubs and weren't averse to giving orders if they deemed it necessary. At best, this meant a good number of people who knew exactly what they were doing and who could keep everyone else on track. At worst, one could get a stalemate as they wrangled over the *right* way to do things. There was a well-known saying — that if you had three archers in one room, you'd get at least four arguments.

On this occasion all seemed to be going well. In a relatively short time, St. John had explained the set-up of the course for the field shoot and had made sure that everyone knew which groups they had been assigned to, how many arrows per target, and how to use the scoring sheets.

'If you're all ready then, we can start. Group one to the front, please, and off you go.'

About ten minutes later, Shaw and Louisa's group got the all-clear to start and they set off.

* * *

After the first round, Shaw decided that Smithy had been right — there were some very tricky shots. One had to have one foot touching a particular post to take each shot and although a few were straightforward, most were at an oblique angle or partially obscured by trees, and the sizes varied depending on the animal target. Most could at least hit the bears, with an above-average number hitting the wolves and the badgers, but the rat and the sparrow proved far more challenging

Everyone had a good time tramping through the wood on a fine spring morning, swapping stories and congratulating or commiserating on each other's shots as appropriate. Louisa got a few very good shots to even out her frequent misses and Shaw did reasonably well throughout, blanking on a few but racking up a respectable score.

As they emerged from the trees for a breather before the second round, Shaw noticed a rather incongruous curly-haired figure leaning on an open gate at the entrance to the wood. The man was wearing perfectly normal outdoor clothes

18

— rather grubby ones, but that was not out of place in itself. Quickly checking him over, he couldn't see any hint of archery-related equipment, which was both unusual and noteworthy as everyone else at the shoot was either carrying or wearing some piece of kit or embellishment, even those he persisted in calling the *non-combatants* — friends or family who were just along for the ride and who often ended up as caddies for the others.

Belatedly, Shaw realised he was staring. The man met his gaze and strode off, heading away from both the shoot and the hotel.

A few minutes later, their group set off once more, scoring better the second time around. Someone even hit the rat.

★   ★   ★

Sitting at a long bench, eating the surprisingly good chilli and bread prepared on site, Shaw and Louisa chatted with the others on their table, swapping experiences from the morning and speculating about the afternoon's event.

'It's listed as a blind 'shoot to the mark'. What exactly is that?' an American woman asked. It was her first time at a British event and she was doing rather well, her style unique, concentrated and deadly accurate.

'Ach, it's easy. The man in charge takes us a' tae a flag or shield or somethin' similar stuck in the grun', which is the mark. Then we a' walk back tae the shootin' line an' take three shots an' ye simply see who's the nearest,' explained a bearded Scottish archer called Will Hazard. He wiped away a lump of steaming chilli which had landed on his jumper.

'Okay, that's pretty straightforward, I guess.'

'There's a catch though,' Hazard continued. 'Once yer back at the line, ye cannae see the mark. It's hidden. Usually they use a bit a grun' that dips doon or sometimes a line o' hay bales or that kind o' thing. Ye'd think that the result would be pretty random, but it's no'. The better archers seem tae zero in on the mark. I once saw a bloke actually split the post wi' his arrow. There was nae need to bring oot the tape measure that time.'

An hour later, the archers reconvened and headed off together along a footpath to a field a short walk away. This was the venue for the blind shoot: a grassy meadow with a stream running down one side and an undulating surface that was proving a little difficult to walk over. Shaw and Louisa found themselves next to the organiser.

'It really is a beautiful spot. Ideal in many ways,' commented St. John. 'And you'd be surprised how easy the whole area has been to adapt. If this weekend goes well I would certainly suggest using Kempshott again.' He pulled his hat down a little to shade his eyes. 'Ah, here we are.'

They came up over a gentle slope and found a dip in the meadow, at the centre of which was a large wooden stake with a shield attached. For the whole of the walk, it hadn't been visible.

St. John hurried to the front of the crowd. 'Right, you can see the mark now. I suggest you have a good look for landmarks you can use to help you and then we'll head back to the shooting line. Scoring is very simple on this one. Three arrows apiece. Closest to the mark wins.'

'I've never done one of these before, Nick. Any tips?' Louisa asked as they made their way back.

'Have you picked a landmark?'

'Yes, some trees a little way back from the mark.'

'Well, it's quite a long distance for you. Two hundred yards perhaps, so I'd suggest you use your flight arrows and give it full draw. It really is a hard one so just give it a go and see what happens.' Shaw counted his arrows. Eleven out of the thirteen he had brought remained. He had broken one and lost one during the field shoot, which was a pretty good outcome overall, considering all the trees he had hit by mistake. Such losses were all part of the course and there was often someone who brought along arrows for sale. Indeed, from the Saturday evening onwards there would be a few tents selling bows, strings, arrows and any number of accessories, and a lively trade would take place.

Eventually they were all lined up and poised to shoot. It always gave Shaw a lift to see the long line of archers ready to start. This was remarkably similar to the way archers down the centuries had practised their skills for battle, and the sight of over a hundred arrows in the air at the same time was very striking. It wasn't quite in the same league as the famous and oft talked about formidable Agincourt *arrowstorm*, but it was impressive all the same.

St. John's gave the command, beginning with: 'Nock thy arrow!' followed by: '*Loose!*' and, accompanied by the hum of many longbow strings, they began.

It would be interesting to see the results, Shaw thought as they began to walk back to the mark. Louisa was annoyed that she had mis-shot one of her arrows and bent to retrieve it. There was friendly chatter among the crowd as they converged on the spot.

'Can I ask you all to keep back while we judge the winner!' St. John bellowed, halting the ones at the front who were a little too eager to see. He and another judge walked carefully among the arrows, making for the mark.

There were a few arrows very close to it, though no one had hit it this time.

After some work with a tape measure, St. John put one hand on the winning arrow, a large black-fletched pine shaft with red threads wound tightly just below the feathers. With some effort, he pulled it free. 'We have a winner! If this is yours please join me with one of your arrows to verify your claim.'

A rangy young man with long hair and a Black Sabbath T-shirt under his jacket loped forward and received a round of applause, winning a few shouts of congratulations from his friends.

'Do you know him?' Louisa asked interestedly.

'Not to speak to, but he's been to one or two events. I think he's Danish. Come on, we can collect our arrows now.'

The next few minutes were taken up with the careful slow walk of people trying not to step on anyone else's arrows as they collected their own. A few had gone long and a handful of people made for the trees set a little way back from the mark.

There was a sudden cry of surprise followed by a shout for St. John.

The organiser rushed over to the small group and then immediately turned back and shouted: 'Are any of you a doctor?'

There was a moment of shocked silence and then Louisa dropped her bow and quiver. 'What's wrong?' she asked as she ran forward. 'I know first aid.'

'I . . . I don't know. There's someone lying in the trees with at least one arrow in them.' St. John's voice was shaky.

Shaw followed more circumspectly, blanching as he saw the arrow protruding from the man's right eye. There was blood all over the face and another arrow had penetrated the unfortunate's left hand. A third arrow protruded from his abdomen.

Louisa lifted an arm and held the wrist, feeling for a pulse.

'He's dead, surely?' Nick asked. 'You couldn't survive that.'

'Got to check properly,' Louisa answered, not flinching as she put her face up against the man's mouth and nose, testing for the

25

slightest hint of breath. She sighed. 'He's definitely gone; completely cold apart from anything else. Which is odd.' She didn't elaborate but stood up and turned to St. John. 'I'm sorry, we're going to have to shut the whole thing down. I'll get the emergency services out here and stay with the body in the meantime.'

St. John was shocked and didn't seem capable of movement.

Louisa put her hand on his arm and said gently: 'This is a suspicious death and it seems likely we'll all need to be questioned.' Reaching into an inside pocket of her jacket, she withdrew a thin wallet and opened it to show him. 'I'm a detective sergeant, Leon. The local force will take over as soon as they get here but for now, I'm in charge and I need you to help keep everyone calm. You too, Nick. Go and tell them that we've found a body. No details yet please.' She gave Shaw a wry, lopsided smile. 'So much for a weekend away from work. Still, I've had a better time than this poor bloke.'

2

Shaw's attempt to write his review of Kempshott House Hotel had been going badly for about forty minutes when Louisa returned, read his effort and replaced it in the bin where it rightly belonged. Once the police had arrived on the scene, the archers had been allowed to wait in the beer tent while the body was examined, photographed and finally removed. As this was happening, the police had begun the lengthy task of taking witness statements from all who had been there — over one hundred people. The only thing that helped was that nearly everyone had the same tale to tell.

Only St. John, Shaw, Louisa and two others had actually seen the body. The rest just knew what they had been told — that a body had been discovered in the spinney forty or so yards behind the mark. For the time being the police, led by Detective Inspector Burrell had requested that the information about the arrows that had hit the body be kept secret. It hadn't stopped speculation amongst the archers though.

'You do realise, I hope, that everyone in the tent was talking about the possibility that one of them could have killed him? It's causing real distress.'

Louisa nodded. 'Of course we do. It's the obvious assumption after all, and I can remember how my heart lurched when I saw that arrow in his eye. For the moment, Burrell wants as little information given out as possible, but there should be an update sometime later this evening.' She flopped into the armchair and pulled off her walking boots. 'That's better! I've been trudging up and down that field for hours.'

'What exactly have you been up to? You're a long way from your patch here,' Shaw asked curiously. He had heard a bit about Louisa's work but she generally preferred to talk about other things.

'I'm unofficial but useful, I think would be the way to put it. I was going to step back as soon as the local police arrived but Burrell asked me to help him understand the setup here. I've a reasonably good alibi for the estimated time of death and I know at least a bit of how the weekend was organised. Leon was very helpful after the first shock wore off, and he's got us a list of all the archers present.'

'There are some extras though; family and friends who weren't competing and so won't be on the list,' Shaw said.

'That information is being added now, hopefully. It's a big job to talk to all of them but everyone's being cooperative at the moment. How that will develop if we have to keep people here past Sunday night . . . well, that might be a different kettle of fish.' She sighed. 'Any chance of a coffee?'

'No trouble.' Shaw turned things over in his mind as he waited for the kettle to boil. 'Louisa, why did you use the word 'alibi' just now? Surely this was an accident?'

She looked at him steadily for a moment. 'If I tell you anything about this that is more than the others are hearing you'll have to be absolutely discrete. Could you manage that?'

Shaw set down the steaming coffee and addressed the question seriously. 'If there are things which you can't tell me, then I respect that and won't ask. If, however, you'd like to be able to discuss this I promise I won't let anything slip. You know I can keep a secret. I've never told any of the archery lot about your job, as requested.' He grinned briefly. 'Leon's face was a picture when you showed him your ID.'

'He adapted quickly though,' Louisa replied. 'He's not the kind who can't relinquish control and he did just what I needed. Look, I would appreciate being able to check a few things over with you. Burrell may ask me for more information about the technicalities of shooting than I know.' She sipped the coffee thoughtfully for a few moments, then began. 'The facts we have at the moment are as follows. The body was discovered by Dave Altringham when he was searching for a lost arrow. Luckily for him, the arrows that had hit the body were not his. The poor guy's in a state of shock as it is. Another archer, Martin Riley, also saw it and it was he who called for Leon. Leon took one look and shouted for a doctor, and you know what happened after that. The body was that of a Caucasian male, early fifties I'd guess, with no visible wounds apart from the arrows in the hand, the guts and the eye.' She put the cup down, reached for a piece of hotel notepaper by the phone and began to sketch. 'This is the mark and the spinney . . . and here is where we found the body. Luckily most of the arrows that were shot didn't have time to be taken out of the ground, so we could see how far the long shots had gone. Only eight had got as far as the spinney, out of over three hundred. Of those eight, five have been identified as belonging to guys who shoot really heavy bows. The other three, the ones that were in the body, belonged to archers who all came up short with their three normal arrows — that is, the ones they'd shot at the mark. In fact, one of them is a junior, Joe Rycroft's son. None of them could

31

shoot far enough to reach the spinney.'

'But how can you say that? Three of those arrows did get far enough. Far enough to hit that poor guy!'

'You don't get it. Each archer shot three arrows to the mark, right? Well the red-and-blue fletched arrow that punctured the man's hand, the black-and-white that was in his stomach and the blue-and-yellow striped one that hit his eye were not shot at the same time as the others. We found three of each of those arrows much further back from the mark. The black and whites were pretty near the mark, but still nowhere near the spinney. What I'm saying is: the dead man wasn't killed by the volley of shots we let off. Something else happened to get those arrows in him, and it looks very much like murder at this point.'

'God! I see what you mean.' Nick was stunned. 'Do you know who the dead man is? I mean did he have a wallet or something?'

'No wallet, no car keys, just the clothes he was wearing. Leon didn't recognise him and he wasn't dressed for archery anyway. I think Burrell was taking the photograph up to the hotel so maybe someone there will recognise him. With the body back at the station they can do fingerprints and take DNA swabs too.' Louisa drained the last of the coffee. 'That only scratched the surface of my need for caffeine. They should do the proper stuff down in the bar. Come on, I want to get an espresso and something to eat before I have to do anything else.' She rose to her feet and pulled her boots back on again with a slight grimace.

They headed downstairs. They were greeted by the sight of Detective Inspector Burrell, who caught sight of Louisa and beckoned them over. 'Sergeant West, I'd appreciate your advice for a few moments.'

'Yes, sir. May I introduce Nicholas Shaw, my partner. He's been attending these kinds of archery events for over fifteen years and may be helpful too.'

Burrell shook Shaw's hand. 'That might be a good idea. I take it you've been interviewed already by one of my officers?'

'That's right. I was with Louisa when she first saw the body.' Shaw looked with interest at the neatly dressed middle-aged man. He wasn't quite what he had imagined a detective inspector would be like. The name Burrell had made him think of a slightly grizzled thick-set man with a scowl, but here was a slim bright-eyed man whose face looked on the verge of a smile most of the time.

'A most unfortunate . . . occurrence if ever there was one,' Burrell acknowledged. 'Anyway, I could do with a coffee, so would you mind accompanying me to the bar? There's an area at the back we've set aside for interviews and it's not being used at the moment.'

'Just where we were heading,' Shaw replied.

Once they were settled, Burrell began. 'I've asked Mr. St. John to assemble his archers in the tent at eight — that's half an hour away. I've an announcement to make which I can summarise for you now. The dead man was *not* killed by any of the arrows that were found in him. I understand that a fair few people have been very upset by the possibility that he was shot by accident and I can set their minds at rest on that point. It does, however, leave us with the only other possibility, which is that he died somewhere else and was brought here. Even then, I don't think that explains the arrows.' He turned to direct his question to Shaw. 'From what Sergeant West has told me, the three that hit him couldn't have been fired in the competition. Would you agree with that, or do you think someone might have fired more than three, either by mistake or on purpose?'

Shaw considered for a moment, picturing the line of archers in his mind. 'I don't think you could rule out the possibility that someone could shoot more arrows than they should have. And, strictly speaking, you don't talk about *firing* arrows. Bullets are fired; arrows are shot.

Burrell smiled and nodded his head in deference. 'I said I was new to this sport. I'll try to remember.'

Shaw continued with his explanation. 'When you're all shooting you tend to concentrate on your own shots rather than anyone else's, and we all shoot at slightly different speeds. Even if you're standing right next to someone you might not notice them shooting four rather than three. What I thought was more telling was that Louisa said that the arrows that hit the man were shot by people who can't usually get that kind of distance.'

'Okay, that fits in with what the preliminary medical report is saying. It looks like the murderer, if there is one, was trying to confuse the evidence by bringing the body here.'

'But, how did the arrows end up hitting him? I still don't get that,' Shaw queried.

'I can think of a way it could have happened,' Louisa volunteered. 'The murderer . . . '

'Better term it *person unknown* at this point,' Burrell interrupted.

'Yes, sir. Well a person or persons unknown could have dumped the body in the spinney, complete with the arrows in it, any time between one and half past two.'

'Why do you narrow it down like that,

and where did they get the arrows?' Burrell asked intently.

'The orphans!' Shaw exclaimed in realisation.

'What?' said Burrell in surprise. 'Where on earth do orphans come into this?'

'That's right, Nick.' Louisa looked approvingly at him, then turned her attention back to Burrell. 'Orphans are what archers commonly call the arrows that get recovered from the field shoot, which happened this morning. If you lose an arrow as you go round you have a quick look for it, but not too long, as you would hold all the groups up. It often happens that another archer will find your arrow and bring it — *the orphaned arrow* — back to the start line. They always set aside an area for orphans, and if you have lost yours you can go and check. Like lost property.'

'The orphans aren't guarded in any way. There's never been a need to do so.' Shaw took up the explanation, seeing the puzzled expression on Burrell's face. 'It would've been very easy to pinch a few arrows from the table, which is near the gate leading to the public footpath. In fact . . . ' He paused, remembering. 'There *was* someone. Louisa, do you remember that man who was watching us when we finished the first round?'

'Yes, I do. I thought he might have been from the brewery, killing some time before the drinking started in the evening.'

'Could be,' Nick conceded. 'But I don't think so. They're usually a friendly lot and this guy definitely didn't give that impression.'

'So correct me if I'm wrong, Mr. Shaw, but this man — or anyone for that matter — could have taken some arrows without being seen, if he or she was lucky. Wouldn't the owners notice?' Burrell was definitely interested in this theory.

'Not necessarily. We all lose or break arrows from time to time and there's no guarantee that they'll be found. Everyone brings spares for that very reason. You could ask the owners of those three arrows if they were missing any by the end of the field shoot this morning.'

'That I will.' Burrell leaned back in his

chair. 'Just before I saw you two, I had a call from the station. They've got a possible ID on the body and we're contacting the next of kin. We might be able to release the information tomorrow morning. As this is an ongoing investigation we may need to ask the archers, all of you, to stay beyond Sunday night. Do you think this is going to cause problems?'

Shaw shared a questioning look with Louisa, then sighed. 'Yes it could, for some. You always get a few who stay on after the official end on Sunday afternoon, though most people pack up and leave fairly soon after the prize-giving. I can pretty much guarantee that the hardcore archers would have stayed the Sunday night, partly to help with the clear-up — in fact most of them are the organisers anyway. It's the foreign contingent who may find it difficult, especially if they have ferry bookings.' He looked worried. 'Do you really think it's likely that one of us had anything to do with this?'

Burrell rose to his feet. 'Frankly I would be surprised, but I can't rule it out. Were you planning to leave on Sunday?'

he asked casually.

'Er, yes actually,' Shaw admitted.

'Might be worth seeing if Mr. Dering has room for you for another night, if the need arises. Thank you for your time. I should head down to address the others now.' Burrell shook hands with Shaw and nodded to Louisa before walking out of the bar.

★ ★ ★

Shaw pondered the detective inspector's parting words as he and Louisa walked down to the beer tent to join the others. Unlike previous years, the atmosphere within the campsite was more than a little subdued, the noise from the beer tent a gentle mutter rather than a cheerful buzz. 'Do you think we're under suspicion?' he finally asked.

Louisa squeezed his hand reassuringly. 'Not really, but he has to think about all the possibilities. I wish we knew who the victim is. That would tell me so much more.'

Shaw looked at her closely. Her fair

hair was caught back in a ponytail and she was flicking the end absently as she walked. Not for the first time, he reflected that she was beautiful when she was absorbed in thought. 'Do you regret that you're not working on this case?' he asked.

'A little,' she admitted. 'It's just the kind of thing I want to do more of. That's why I joined the police to begin with. I'd probably be feeling different though if it looked like one of our friends was mixed up in it.'

'They could be, you know,' Shaw remarked frankly. He hadn't wanted to allow the thought to form, but he could not completely dismiss the possibility.

'Well, until the name of the deceased is released there's nothing much to link anyone with the death. We still don't know for sure if it was murder.' They had reached the entrance to the beer tent and squashed into the crowded space.

'Not a moment too soon,' Shaw commented as he saw Burrell taking up a position at one end. 'I'll try to get us a drink. What do you want?'

'I'll take pot luck. Just choose the one with the strangest name,' Louisa replied, her eyes on the detective inspector.

Burrell began to speak, explaining that he didn't think it was the arrows that had caused the man's death. There was a collective sigh of relief, then a lot of murmurings.

Here we go, thought Shaw as he made his way back to Louisa with two pints of Old Knobbler. Sure enough, a moment later a loud voice rang out.

'So if none of our arrows killed the poor bugger, what did?' That was Smithy, channelling the thoughts of all assembled.

'As yet, I'm not at liberty to say,' Burrell answered. 'We've more work to do on this and I'm afraid that I'll have to ask for your continued assistance and patience. I've liaised with Mr. St. John about tomorrow's . . . ' He consulted a piece of paper. ' . . . flight shoot, and I see no reason why it can't go ahead. The proposed site for it is well away from the scene of the crime.' The murmurings were sounding more favourable now. 'However, I may have to ask you to postpone your departure a little. I'm sure you would rather we complete all the questions here instead of having to follow up later at your homes, and I would prefer to talk with you while this is all still fresh in your minds.'

Shaw scanned the room surreptitiously to see how people were taking this news. The mood seemed to be one of resignation. He guessed that what they wanted most of all was for things to return to normal.

St. John cleared his throat. 'I'm sure I speak for us all when I say that we've been deeply shocked by this turn of events. We understand that you need to investigate and will do everything to help you.'

'Thank you,' Burrell replied. 'I don't think we're likely to need you more tonight, so I will leave you in peace for now. I'd ask that if any of you remembers something that might relate to the death, please let me or one of my officers know.' He left the tent with a nod to the crowd.

For a moment there was silence, then St. John spoke again. 'As the detective inspector has been kind enough to allow our shoot tomorrow to continue, I suggest that we try to carry on with our weekend as best we can, but I propose a minute's silence while we pay our respects to the dead.'

Throughout the tent heads bowed as they honoured the unknown man whose death would forever be linked with the memory of this time and place. When they resumed their conversations it was in low tones. Louisa tugged gently on Shaw's hand and led him out of the tent.

A few feet away, Burrell was talking with one of his uniformed officers. A moment later he turned towards them. 'I wish all our witnesses were as co-operative as this lot. Not a real complaint from any of them so far.'

'Well, there are worse places to be detained in than a tent with beer, food and a fair number of your friends,' Shaw commented, raising a smile from Burrell. 'More seriously, I think we'd all like to know what really happened here today. To leave now would feel unfinished some-how.'

'Whatever the reason, I'm grateful. I'll

be back in the morning.' With that, Burrell bade them goodnight.

★   ★   ★

Later, much later, Shaw and Louisa walked back to the hotel. It was a beautiful night and most people's initial reluctance to enjoy the evening had worn off after a while. They noticed that a few off-duty members of the hotel staff, including Dering's niece, Stephanie, had brought down plates of sausages and bread rolls and then stayed to join in. The main topic of conversation had of course been the punctured body. The normal talk of arrows, strings and real ale, mingled with a generous amount of catching up, seemed periodically to erupt into increasingly wild speculation.

'I've heard more ridiculous theories about this murder than I'd have thought possible,' Louisa said, linking her arm through Shaw's. 'I think the prize for the most outrageous has to go to that Dutch guy, the one with his own tankard.'

'What was it again?' Shaw was finding

it difficult to walk. He had sampled all of the beers on offer several times, as well as some of the home-made cider, and he was beginning to regret his decision not to camp. The thought of just rolling from the bar into his sleeping bag was feeling very tempting right now.

'He said that the dead man was probably out collecting magic mushrooms. Where he got that idea from, God only knows.' Feeling Shaw wobble worryingly, she took a firmer grip on his arm. 'Come on, soldier. Time for bed. I've got to be on the ball tomorrow, even if you haven't.'

'Sleuthing, eh?'

'Perhaps.' Louisa steered Shaw back to the welcoming lights of Kempshott House. 'Or maybe I want to win the flight shoot.' Whichever was the truer statement, the look of determination in her eyes spelled trouble for someone. 'Have you seen Mr. Dering today?' she suddenly asked.

'The hotel owner? No, don't think so. Why?' Shaw managed to answer.

Louisa looked at his rapidly glazing

eyes. 'I wondered how he's taking all this — hating it or loving it? You never know.'

A short stagger later, Louisa poured Shaw into bed and stood for a while with the lights off, gazing out of the window.

3

'Come on, Nick! Wake up!'

Shaw stirred as he felt Louisa's warm breath on his face. The curtains were drawn back, letting the sunlight in, somewhat painfully for his eyes.

'I want to see if I can catch Mr. Dering before breakfast. I've a few ideas about that field.'

Shaw moaned gently. The mild throbbing at his temples was making itself felt.

'A nice bath, strong tea and a cooked breakfast will sort you out,' Louisa announced. 'Just think how much worse Smithy and Jason will be feeling. They drank more than you and don't have a nice warm hotel bed to doss down in. Just imagine that first trip to the portaloo and count yourself lucky.'

Shaw had to concede that she had a point. Without exception, all communal portaloos stank like nothing on earth, nothing wholesome anyway. In addition they were not for the claustrophobic and had a tendency to lurch unnervingly for no apparent reason.

A little later, after a bath and cup of tea, he felt ready to tackle the day. Louisa had already gone downstairs when he came out of the bathroom so he pulled on his clothes and set off to find her — or failing that, to at least find breakfast.

The dining room was busy and he recognised quite a few faces. Here and there a coat slung over the back of someone's chair indicated that they were campers who had decided to have breakfast in comfort. He spotted Louisa and was slightly surprised to see her sitting with none other than Dering himself.

'Good morning, Mr. Shaw. This lovely lady has been keeping me company.' The owner called a waiter over to take Shaw's order and poured him out a cup of excellent coffee. 'I understand that the archery is still to go ahead and I'm very pleased to hear it. I had feared that the police would call a halt.'

'DI Burrell saw no reason to do so,'

Louisa said mildly. 'Nick, I was just asking Mr. Dering about the footpaths that crisscross his land.'

'So you were. There are several and I can assure you that signs were put up at each and every one. I checked them all personally. I know Mr. St. John and Mr. Bridges told me that they had done it, but as the landowner I felt obliged to be sure.'

'I don't suppose *you* know who the dead man was?' Shaw asked interestedly. The coffee was reviving him nicely and he almost felt on for the fry-up he had ordered.

'No idea. At first the police wanted me to see the body in case I recognised him, and I'd steeled myself to do it — then all of a sudden they changed their minds. Said it wouldn't be necessary. I suppose that means they've identified the poor soul?' He looked enquiringly at Louisa.

'Possibly,' she answered casually. 'Mr. Dering, do you know if the people living locally were aware of this weekend's tournament? Was it common knowledge?'

'Well, a fair few will have heard about it. I've had a flyer up in the local shops for about a month just in case any locals were into bows and arrows, and I employed some of the lads to help us get the campsite mown and sorted out. I bring them in on occasions, like when we do weddings.' Dering considered for a moment. 'Yes, I would say that most of the village would have known, one way or another.'

'And have you had any complaints about it?' she asked.

'Only one, and that was a half-hearted affair. Jimmy Threlfall came to have a word with me about it. He used to be the gamekeeper when Kempshott was a private house. He's a good sort and we've had a few talks about reintroducing pheasants and such like to the woods. He got worried that if this archery became a regular thing it would put the kibosh on his pheasants. I put him right about that — I don't see why we couldn't do both, I told him. Just a case of scheduling the archery for a time when it wouldn't worry the birds.'

'If he used to work here before it was a hotel, then he must be a little long in the tooth. I thought this had been a hotel for a while,' Shaw said moments before his breakfast arrived.

'Not that long really. About five years. I only took on the hotel last year and just recently managed to buy back the land that had been sold off from the original estate. The Landry family had it before that for a while but I don't think they did a very good job. The old place was very run down. Nearly broke Mrs. Norden's heart, it did.'

Dering poured himself some fresh coffee and seemed perfectly happy to chat with them, but Shaw could see Louisa keeping a surreptitious eye on the time. Stirring in a heaped teaspoon of amber sugar crystals, he continued: 'The Nordens were the last family to own Kempshott outright. They're an offshoot of the Percevals, as Mrs. Norden never fails to remind people. She had to sell the house in the end as she just couldn't afford the running costs. You'd have to be as rich as Croesus these days to have a house like this as a private residence. Mrs. Norden lives in a cottage on the grounds and comes up sometimes to see the place. She was very unimpressed with the way the Landrys ran it, and let them know on several occasions, but they couldn't get rid of her.' He grinned at the memory. 'She's losing it a bit these days but back then when she sold Kempshott she ring-fenced a little plot of land with her cottage and garden on it. It's totally separate from the estate.

'It was actually she who put me on to this place to begin with. I used to run a small hotel over in Staithe, about ten miles from here. A nice old building with a bit of character. It seems Margaret Norden knew the Landrys were close to giving up on Kempshott so she did a bit of research, visiting hotels to see if she approved of their style. One day this determined old lady booked in for a weekend and proceeded to make life very difficult for us. She was into everything: the kitchens, the laundry room, nipping into other guests' rooms when the chambermaid was cleaning them. We coped with the invasion pretty well and on the Sunday afternoon she tracked me down in the office and put her proposal to me. 'I quite like the way you run your hotel, Mr. Dering. You have a feel for history and good service,' she said, telling me about Kempshott.'

'I can't help feeling a little sorry for the Landrys. She sounds formidable!' Louisa commented.

'Well, they had their chance. Once I saw Kempshott — and more importantly, saw Margaret's photographs of how it used to be — I just had to buy it, and I'm glad I did. It took me a while to fix everything up and claw back the land. Margaret helped with that too. She's well in with all of the farmers round here and persuaded them to sell at reasonable rates.' Dering spread his arms wide, encompassing the splendid dining room filled with customers. 'And here we are today! Margaret's happy that her old home is well loved and well looked after, and I have a beautiful and reasonably profitable hotel.'

'What does Mrs. Norden make of us lot descending on Kempshott?' Shaw asked, a memory stirring in his mind.

Dering's smile faded a little and lost some of its gleam. 'Well I'll be honest with you, she rather took against the idea at first, and I'm afraid that this last year she's started to be a bit forgetful and confused. We had some trouble with her when she saw the campsite from her bedroom window. Stephanie — that's my niece who I believe you've already met — is very fond of Margaret and had a brainwave. She found out about the — what was it? The Royal Company of Archers: a centuries-old, established regimental order that serve as ceremonial bodyguards to the monarch while they're in Scotland. Lots of pictures of proper gentlemen carrying bows and suchlike. Margaret is a terrible snob and that swung it for her. If it's good enough for the queen, it's good enough for her!'

So that was the explanation of the exchanges he and Smithy had heard on the Friday night, Shaw thought.

'I didn't see any cottage near the campsite,' Louisa commented sharply.

'You'd be hard pressed to do so. It's well hidden behind that little wood, and the thatched roof blends in.'

'If you'll excuse me, I need to make a call. I've enjoyed our talk, Mr. Dering.' Louisa stood up and hurried away.

Dering stared after her in bewilderment. 'Did I say something wrong?'

'I don't think so, but you may have said something important. You do know Louisa is a police officer?' Shaw queried as he used his last piece of toast to clean his plate.

'Yes, she introduced herself as such this morning. No false pretences.' Dering leaned forward, settling his elbows among the breakfast plates. 'I don't mind telling you that I would like this business cleared up quickly. I know some people say it's all good publicity, but I don't think I'd want the kind of guests who would come here because of it.'

His mention of false pretences gave Shaw a slight pang of guilt. He decided it was his turn to come clean. 'Did Louisa happen to mention my profession?' he asked slightly awkwardly.

'No. You're not a detective as well?' Dering raised his eyebrows. Obviously

Shaw didn't strike him as the type.

'Not as such, although I am inquisitive to the point of nosiness, which Louisa once said was a prerequisite for her job as well.' Shaw took the plunge. 'I'm a travel writer, a hotel reviewer.'

Dering looked surprised for a second, then broke into a slightly wry smile. 'Well, I will take heart from the fact that you've almost taken the pattern off your plate.'

Shaw nodded his head. 'Your food, so far, has been first-class; and to be honest, the prices you charge will keep away simple thrill-seekers.'

Dering threw back his head and laughed, the warm sound adding to the gentle buzz of contented eaters. 'I like that, Mr. Shaw. I like that.'

★ ★ ★

Shaw caught up with Louisa at the entrance to the hotel. 'Any news?' he asked.

'Some,' she answered laconically.

When it was clear that she wasn't going to add to the statement, Shaw changed tack. 'I confessed all to Dering.'

'What!' She turned to him, startled for a second.

'About being a hotel reviewer. He took it well.'

'Oh, I see. Sorry, Nick, but I need to talk to DI Burrell when he gets here. I may miss the flight shoot.'

'You'll be fine. I know the timetable says it starts at ten but I've never known it to be on time. I usually hear the organiser's klaxon as I'm still curled up in my tent.' He put his arm around her waist. 'It would be nice if you can make it. You've got a real chance with those new tapered arrows.'

Louisa turned around and returned the hug affectionately. 'I'll make it if I can, but I can't pass up the opportunity I have here. DI Burrell has let me tag along and it's the most interesting case I've had the chance to work on yet. I'm worried that none of us knew about Margaret Norden and her cottage. She might have seen something yesterday and no one has interviewed her.'

'Is that what you rushed away to sort out?'

'Yes. That, and to see if they've confirmed the cause of death.'

'And?'

'I can't say yet, I'm sorry. DI Burrell might release the details later this morning and then you'll all know. Though I'm fairly confident that none of the archers had anything to do with it. Anyway, I'm going to wait here. You go.'

'All right, but I'm taking your kit with me just in case,' Shaw said.

A few minutes later she was still waiting as he carried both bows and sets of arrows. She was on her mobile.

Shaw raised a bow in farewell and walked down to the campsite. As he had predicted, by ten minutes to ten there was only a poor showing of participants. St. John walked to the centre of the tents, a fine assortment of big and small, modern and wonderfully archaic — particularly the medieval-style round tent complete with pennant flag flying.

The klaxon blared horribly and St. John raised his voice to shout: 'Flight shoot to start in ten minutes. If you want to take part you need to come to the starting line pretty damn quick!'

It had the desired effect as by ten-thirty a good number of people had lined up ready to compete. Not as many as the day before, but that was usual. There were always a few for whom Sunday morning was a blur. No sign of Louisa either, Shaw realised with a slight feeling of disappointment. On the occasions where they had practised the long shots she had been doing really well. Her bow was only a fifty-pound draw-weight, but that didn't matter for this event. She could well have won the women's competition. At the end of the day the flight shoot was really just a question of who could shoot the furthest. There was technique but no real accuracy involved. It depended more on the equipment used than the user.

The shoot went as planned, with no unpleasant discoveries this time. Smithy did well as always, after a rushed awakening, and came second, but the honours for the men went to a Welsh archer, Tom Williams.

Shaw found himself next to Williams as they collected their arrows. 'That was some nice work,' he said, congratulating the other. 'What did you get?'

'Two hundred and seventy-eight yards. Not bad into wind. It's rather satisfying as this is my first time at a competition,' the long-armed Welshman replied. 'As long as the wife doesn't hear about the corpse, it won't be my last. She'd freak out about it.'

'It doesn't normally happen, you know,' Shaw answered with mock anxiety.

'That's what makes it so strange. Why here, why now? Is there a connection?'

Williams turned and walked back to the starting line, leaving Shaw pondering his words. He had been assuming that the only connection between the body and the archers was an opportunistic and none-too-bright theft of the arrows, but was he just hoping that was the case? He felt a sudden need to find Louisa, to put his mind at rest or else find out the truth. Rapidly, he sent a text to her phone: *Any news?* he typed, then waited impatiently for an answer. After about a minute his mobile beeped. *Lots. Meet me at hotel.* He didn't need a second prompt and strode quickly back.

The police were there in force and were obviously searching the hotel thoroughly. DI Burrell was nowhere to be seen but Louisa was waiting in the foyer. 'We've released a statement to the press. Have a look.' She handed Shaw a sheet of A4 headed paper.

He scanned it quickly, skipping the formal language to get to the pertinent facts. 'John Francis Fullerton . . . So that's the victim.' He moved further down the page. 'Christ! They think he was shot? By an actual bullet?'

'That's right. After the autopsy, the pathologist confirmed his initial thoughts. Fullerton was killed by a gunshot wound to the abdomen. A low-calibre bullet so that the wound was not very deep. Someone then managed to retrieve the bullet and tried to disguise the wound by digging an arrow into it. The other two arrows seem to have been added for verisimilitude — to make it look more like the arrows had caused his death.' Louisa was talking quietly, walking to the empty drawing room.

'It's possible that the shot was accidental, but even then there's conspiracy to pervert the course of justice and of course it's far more likely that it was a premeditated crime.'

Shaw sat down heavily on the nearest sofa, feeling rather sick. 'I don't know why, but the fact that he was shot has really shocked me.'

'I'm not surprised. You've never had anything to do with a gun. I don't think you've ever handled one, have you?

'You're right, I haven't. I'm sorry, Louisa. I'm being stupid.' His face looked rather pale.

'Well, you are now. Don't apologise for being a decent human being, for God's sake! We *should* be shocked by a violent death. I have to see it as part of my job but I wouldn't want you to be blasé about it. Stay here, I'll be back in a moment.' Louisa returned quickly with a glass of iced water and insisted he take a few sips. 'No doubt the news will have got to the others by now.'

'How? They're in the middle of a field.'

'I know your mobile is almost old enough to be steam-powered, but anyone with a smart phone will have been able to pick this up. Right now, I want to go down and see what the effect of this information has been on them. You never know, someone might have heard a shot at some point.'

'Have they got a time of death?'

'Yes, early morning on Saturday — between about seven and ten. I can also tell you now that when forensics examined the area where the body was discovered, they found only a small amount of blood. However there is a rough track about four hundred metres away, and at the edge of the track there were traces of blood on the ground. Looks like Fullerton was shot there and then moved.'

'And all this was going on while people were in the campsite!' Shaw raked his fingers through his tousled hair and then abruptly stood up. 'I think some fresh air would do me good. Come on, let's head down there.'

'Right. I can tell you the rest on the way.' Louisa took the press release and folded it into an inner pocket in her jacket.

'There's more?'

'Oh yes, but wait until we've left the hotel.' Once they were past the beautifully mown lawns and flower-filled borders and moved on to the rougher path, she continued. 'John Fullerton lived about eight miles away in Broughton and listed himself as a self-employed accountant. We identified him, however, by his finger-prints.'

'He was a criminal?' Shaw exclaimed in surprise

Louisa rocked her hand in the air to indicate uncertainty. 'He was arrested a few years ago on suspicion of fraud, but was later released and has had no further contact with the police. The interesting point is that he was working for a Mr. Michael Landry at the time.' Seeing the spark of recognition in his face, she nodded. 'Yes. The same Landry who ran Kempshott before Dering.'

Shaw glanced back towards the hotel. 'Has he been told yet? Dering, I mean?'

'Burrell's interviewing him again right now. There are a few questions that he has to answer.'

Although she had spoken lightly, Shaw latched onto the words. 'Are you saying that Dering's a suspect?' he asked incredulously.

'Actually, no. That's not Burrell's angle at the moment. There's something odd about the whole thing, I mean odder than it already is. According to Mrs. Fullerton, who made a positive identification of the body early this morning, her husband had left the house on Friday night to attend a business meeting early on Saturday. As a matter of fact, she hadn't believed his story and suspected him of having an affair, but that may not be relevant. His car's still missing and we don't have any idea what happened to him after he left home. He didn't die until the following morning so he must have spent the night somewhere. As there is a connection between Fullerton and Dering, albeit a loose one, Burrell's asking Dering more about the Landry-Fullerton fraud business, to see if he knows anything.'

Louisa had slowed her pace, clearly wanting to finish the conversation before they reached the campsite. Looking to her right, she saw a large tree stump, the only remains of what must have been a huge tree. 'Sit down here for a minute, Nick, will you?' She perched on the stump. 'We didn't find a wallet on Fullerton; you know that already. All he had in his pockets was a bit of loose change and a scrap of paper. It just read, 'Saturday, seven-fifteen.' Nothing else.'

'You said Dering's not a suspect, at least not yet. If you start to add up the fact that Fullerton is connected to Landry and Kempshott, surely the possibility must have crossed your mind at some point?'

'Everything crosses my mind when I'm working,' Louisa answered dryly. 'However, Dering has a very good alibi, as it happens. He was having an early breakfast with several of the hotel staff from six in the morning and then going over the day's duties with the deputy manager at the reception desk. After that he was in and around the hotel with one person or another until lunchtime. Unless someone killed Fullerton on his orders, he's in the clear.' She looked at her watch and saw that it was just after twelve. 'Let's go on

67

now. I texted Leon earlier and asked to see him at half past twelve.' She stood up, looking for a second at the view. Kempshott House was at the crest of a small hill, with the surrounding fields laid out below it. She pointed to the edge of the wood where they had first shot. 'Look! You can just about make out the edge of Margaret Norden's cottage among the trees, but you'd have to be looking for it.'

The thatched roof was only just visible and Shaw wasn't at all surprised that they hadn't noticed it before.

'Louisa!' came a shout from nearby. They turned to see St. John striding towards them.

'I got your text and thought it might be better to talk away from the others.'

'Thanks, Leon. I wanted to ask you about the time you came to check this place out for the shoot. When would that have been?'

'Why, it was back in October. Kendrick had been looking around for somewhere and got to hear about Kempshott. I think the owner, Mr. Dering, had been putting out feelers to various sports clubs, offering it as a venue. I came over and met with Kendrick and Smithy and we had a tour of the place.'

'Did you know about the little cottage near the field-shoot wood?' Louisa asked, pointing it out for him.

'No, I didn't,' responded St. John, shaking his head. He looked worried.

She turned her back on the view. 'How are the others today — particularly the three whose arrows were stolen?'

'Mostly all right, I think, but I'm sure they would like to know just what happened. Young Rycroft is actually quite excited about it all, now that it's been established that they didn't kill the man by accident. Fairly normal response for a twelve-year-old boy I suppose. There were a few of the inevitable comments last night. Nothing too irreverent.' St. John scratched his well-groomed beard speculatively. 'Any news on whether we can leave tonight?'

'I don't know yet, Leon. Are you in a hurry to get away?' She managed to ask this without sounding suspicious.

'I'm fine. I was going to stay on tonight

in any case. We'd planned to have a bit of a discussion about the weekend and sort out possible dates for next year. I've been asking around and I'd say that a little under half of the people here would be facing difficulties if they have to stay longer.'

'I had an idea about that,' Shaw said. He'd been turning it over in his mind as the others talked. 'I know that the clout shoot after lunch was going to be the last event. If Burrell does keep us here, do you think it would possible to set up something else for the late afternoon?'

'What kind of thing did you have in mind?' St. John asked curiously.

Shaw rapidly ran over several options in his mind. 'How about a speed shoot? We could probably cadge a bottle of whisky from Dering as a prize.'

'Good idea, Nick. I'll keep that as a card up my sleeve in case we need it.' St. John looked back towards the campsite where the crowd was milling around, chatting and browsing among the three stalls that had been set up. 'I'll head back and have a word with Kendrick and

Smithy. Are you coming?'

'Soon. Thanks, Leon,' Louisa said. She turned back to look down on the fields. From where they were she could see the area taken up by the archery. The campsite was the closest to the hotel, with the two fields beyond it; one had been used for the ill-fated blind shoot, and the other was where the flight competition had just happened. The wooded area swept off to the right and they could just make out the track which ran along the back of the fields and where Fullerton had, in all likelihood, been killed. 'There's someone out there who used this beautiful place to end a life. Who purposefully dragged a lot of decent people into a murder.' She spoke softly but with feeling.

Shaw put his arm round her shoulders. 'You'll get them, I'm sure of it.'

They stood together in silence.

Suddenly Shaw noticed a plume of smoke rising from the wood. An instant later, he grabbed Louisa's hand and started running down the slope.

'What is it? What are you doing?' she shouted.

'The cottage — it's on fire! Someone call the fire brigade!' They were nearly at the gate to the campsite now. He could see St. John chatting to Kendrick. 'Leon!' he yelled. 'That cottage in the wood is on fire and an old woman lives there!' Without waiting for a response, he plunged into the trees with Louisa hot on his heels.

4

Shaw could smell the smoke now as well as see it, rising up above the wood. He had no other idea of how to reach the cottage than to break a way through the trees. He could hear the sound of other feet crashing through the dense bracken behind him but didn't waste time by calling out. The thought of anyone being stuck in the burning house galvanised him and he raced on. After about four breathless minutes, he saw the trees thin out and become a small glade with Margaret Norden's cottage in the centre.

He had not been mistaken. The fire had taken hold of the upper floor and partially burned through the thatch already. He ran across the lawn and tried to open the door. It was locked. 'Mrs. Norden! Are you there?' he hollered as he ran round to the windows, looking through each in turn. At the third one he saw her — a small shape on the floor in the kitchen.

Cursing with fear, he completed the circuit of the cottage and found a back door, but it too was shut fast. He started to look around for something he could use to break in with.

'Nick! Where are you?' It was Smithy's booming voice.

Shaw felt a huge surge of relief. 'Over here! There's a woman in the kitchen!' he shouted back.

Smithy, Kendrick and what seemed like a horde of others came running. Smithy took one look at the door then raised a booted foot. He crashed it into the door, making it shake, but the door held. He swore and kicked again. This time the door gave way with a splintering crash. A blast of heat and thick black smoke poured out, causing them to pull back.

'We've got to get her out quickly. God knows how much longer the ceiling's going to stay up,' shouted Shaw, raising his voice above the horribly loud sound of the burning cottage.

He stepped through the ruined door and immediately felt his throat constrict. There was an acrid smell and although the smoke had only just started to penetrate the ground floor, it stung his eyes badly. He turned into the kitchen and leaned down to grab the old woman. Getting his hands under her arms, he managed to drag her inert body to the hallway. The smoke was thickening now and he didn't want to stand up, taking his face into the black greasy air near the ceiling. Screwing his eyes almost shut, he dragged her towards the doorway and felt another's hands guiding him out.

'We've got her, Nick. We need to get away from the house.' It was Louisa. She and Kendrick picked up Mrs. Norden.

Shaw joined them as they hurried across the back lawn to where a group of people were standing, watching helplessly as the fire raged. Even from this distance the heat was intense. 'I don't see Smithy.'

'He's checking inside,' Louisa answered, her voice tight with concern. 'I called the fire brigade but the only access to this place is that track that runs behind the fields. They won't be able to get here very quickly.' She had a first-aid box beside her and was searching through it for anything useful.

A shout came from the cottage and they both looked up fearfully. Smithy emerged, crawling on all fours. He had his shirt wrapped around his nose and mouth and was pulling something behind him. Black smoke billowed out of the doorway, much lower than it had been when Shaw had been inside. St. John and Kendrick dashed over and helped Smithy pull the scorched form of a second woman from the flaming cottage. The large, strong man crawled a little further and then stopped, breaking out into a severe coughing fit.

St. John took over the burden of the second victim, carefully lifting and carrying her back to the group.

With an ear-splitting crash, the roof collapsed in a whirling chaos of fiery beams and red hot embers. Falling inwards, it smashed through the bedroom floor to the rooms below. A huge exclamation came from the onlookers as the unconfined flames leaped even higher.

'Susie, can you stay with this lady? I think she's only unconscious. Check her breathing,' Louisa delegated hastily. She picked up the first-aid box and ran to the other casualty.

Shaw felt his stomach contract ominously. This other woman appeared to be a bit younger than Mrs. Norden — in her sixties, he would guess. There was blood on her head and running down her face, but the thing which was making him gag was the awful suppurating burn on her left leg.

'Is she breathing?' Louisa tersely asked St. John, who had carefully placed her in the recovery position.

'I think so,' he replied. 'I felt a pulse anyway.' He wiped his forehead with his sleeve and burst out: 'When are the bloody services going to get here? She could be dying!'

'They've got to bring the vehicles round the back. I told them to get paramedics to the campsite and we could direct them from there. Lars and Karin stayed back to meet them.' Louisa found a large packet that contained a cooling gel patch for burns. She unpeeled it and carefully applied it to the woman's leg.

'I can hear sirens!' Shaw exclaimed.

They sounded a long way off, but thankfully a moment later there was a shout as two paramedics came out of the wood accompanied by Lars. He had been dressed in his usual Viking gear for the shoot and looked strangely at home running through the trees. The paramedics immediately took responsibility for the two injured women and a few minutes later a team of fire-fighters arrived.

Shaw suddenly felt the horror and exertion catching up with him. Everyone was moved back to the track where the fire engine was and watched as the water pelted down onto the burning cottage. They had located a stream nearby which was still high from last year's wet winter and switched to that when the water tank dried up. It seemed to take a monumental amount of hosing to put the fire out.

In the meantime Shaw and Louisa, both surplus to requirements for the time being, sat numbly on the grass verge of the track.

'My God. If you hadn't seen the fire they'd both be dead,' Louisa said after a while. 'The smoke or the collapse of the roof would have most certainly killed them.'

'What happened when I ran off? I can't remember,' Shaw asked dazedly.

'You yelled to Leon about the fire and set off as if the hounds of Hell were after you. Kendrick and Smithy heard as well. They dropped everything and followed you. Leon ran to get the first-aid box, sensible man. I called the emergency services and got Lars and Karin to wait for them to arrive. Then I followed Leon.' Louisa looked round at the crowd of thirty or so people and smiled shakily. 'I guess word got round pretty fast.'

They sat in silence for a while, then saw a procession coming towards the ambulance that was parked next to the fire engine. The paramedics, with the help of two fire-fighters, were carrying the still-unconscious women on stretchers. As they drew level with the crowd one of the paramedics went to Smithy, whose eyes were still streaming either from smoke or emotion.

'You'd better come along too. I want to check you for smoke inhalation.'

Smithy didn't object but climbed

dutifully into the ambulance.

'Thank heavens for that,' Louisa sighed. 'I asked them to look him over and I thought he might resist.'

A black car came bumping down the track and drew to a halt. Dering flung open the door and almost fell out. 'Margaret! Oh God . . . and Janice too!' he cried, seeing the two women strapped into the stretchers. 'What the hell happened here?'

St. John hurried over to explain to the distraught man.

Another figure exited the car — Detective Inspector Burrell. He stood in conversation with the firemen for a few moments, staring towards the ruined cottage with a stony expression. The ambulance pulled away, heading for the nearest hospital. He looked around at the gathered crowd. Seeing Louisa, he strode over. 'Are you all right, Sergeant West?' he addressed her formally.

She shook herself out of the semi-stupor that both she and Shaw had descended into. 'Fine, sir. Just a bit shocked.'

'Not surprising, given the circumstances. I've got approval for your formal secondment to my team for the duration of this investigation. My usual man is off with flu and you already know this case. If you're up to it, I'd like you to start now.'

Louisa got to her feet. 'Thank you, I'd like that very much.' She turned to Shaw. 'You okay now, Nick?' she asked.

Shaw paused for a moment before replying. He was exhausted and felt emotionally drained by the dramatic rescue. 'This was attempted murder, wasn't it?' He directed his question to Burrell, who pursed his lips and tried to fudge an answer, but Shaw was having none of it. 'I saw the wounds on both those women's heads. I've still got Margaret Norden's blood on my clothes. Someone hit them, knocking them unconscious, and then set the house on fire.' He wearily pulled himself up, taking Louisa's offered arm. 'I'm very far from being okay, but I'll be better knowing that you're doing everything you can to find the bastard who did this.'

Louisa said nothing but caught Shaw in a brief, fierce embrace before leaving with Burrell to discuss their next moves.

Dering, barred from going in the ambulance due to lack of space, had been standing a little way off from Shaw when the exchange had taken place. Now he moved closer and they stood watching the ragged plume of smoke that was dissipating now the fire crew had put the conflagration out. He suddenly blurted out, his voice cracked and impassioned: 'She's a good girl, your Louisa, and Burrell seems to know his stuff, but I'll tell you one thing. After what I saw today, they'd damn well better find whoever did this before I do.'

Shaw looked at the distressed, shell-shocked and, in many cases, angry faces of those who had run to help and witnessed the dreadful scenes. He thought Dering was not the only one who felt that way. In his own heart he could feel a new coldness that he knew was reserved solely for the murderer of Fullerton and the would-be murderer of two defenceless old women.

* * *

The mood in the archery campsite was very subdued that afternoon. A few people had stayed to watch the fire finally being extinguished, but by three o'clock everyone was gathered in loose groups, waiting to see if they would need to stay the night.

Dering had asked Shaw to come with him to the campsite to see how people were and if they needed anything. 'I know most of you had planned to leave around now and I'd like to be able to help,' he said.

'You know, what might be really good would be the opportunity to have a decent wash. I know when I'm camping that's the thing I miss most, and some of us got pretty messed up in the fire,' Shaw answered.

'Of course! There are currently three empty rooms. If someone would like to organise a rota for those who would like a shower, I'm more than happy to give them the keys.' Dering cheered up a little at the prospect. Shaw knew he had tried to get information about Margaret and Janice from the hospital, but as he wasn't a relation they wouldn't tell him anything.

They wandered round the site until

Shaw saw Karin. She had changed into modern clothes and at first he hadn't recognised her. They discussed Dering's offer and Karin declared it a great idea. 'You leave it to me. I'll bring those interested up to the hotel in half an hour if that's all right.'

'Right. I'll nip back and get things sorted, extra towels and the like.' Dering looked Shaw up and down. 'I think you should come with me. You'd definitely benefit from a wash and a change of clothes.'

Shaw abruptly remembered that he was bloodstained and blackened by the smoke. It hadn't seemed to matter, but now he felt a pressing need to be clean again.

They walked up to the hotel, passing the place where he had first spotted the fire. Shaw paused there. He could just make out yellow-helmeted blurs beneath the tree cover. The firemen had turned investigators now, searching for clues as to how the fire had been started.

'I just can't believe anyone would do such a thing,' Dering said quietly. His hands were thrust in his pockets and his normally jovial face was drawn.

Shaw thought back to his conversation with Louisa on this spot. It seemed like an age ago already. She had said that the dead man was connected with Kempshott. 'Did the police tell you about their identification of the shot body?' he asked cautiously.

'Yes! We were discussing Fullerton and his shenanigans when Burrell got a call about the fire. When I heard it was the cottage, I insisted he drive me there. John Fullerton was a rogue. No doubt about it. He and Michael Landry tried every trick in the book to make the hotel look more profitable than it was at the time. I'd heard of massaging the figures before but these two put the numbers through a day-long spa treatment!'

Dering turned and led Shaw back up to the hotel, talking as he went. 'I recognised a few of their dodges but I still would have paid over the odds if Margaret hadn't been so canny. She went through the books with me, checking every detail and comparing them with her observations and the information she got from the other staff.' Seeing Shaw's look of surprise, Dering nodded his head. 'Yes, she got friendly with some of the maids. Asked them to tea at the cottage from time to time. I think at first she wanted to keep a connection with her home, but as time went on she realised that Landry and his wife Elaine were cutting corners everywhere. She didn't like that one bit and when she heard that Landry was planning to sell off the furniture he had bought with the house she stormed off to complain. You see, she sold Kempshott with various provisos — one of which was that the house and contents had to be kept together. She hadn't been able to stop him selling the fields as that had not been specified, but when it came to her family's furniture she had him.'

They'd reached the hotel and Dering ushered Shaw into the bar, where he poured him a large glass of whisky. 'Get that inside you. You look like you need it. Anyway, Margaret read the Landrys the riot act. Said she would set her lawyers on them if they sold so much as a cushion. They argued terribly. Landry said that they couldn't make money as a hotel and wanted to sell it to a developer to be made into flats. Margaret insisted, quite rightly, that the clause in the deeds of the property required her agreement for any substantial change to be made to the building and that it was a listed building anyway. One of my maids worked here at the time and said it was a real blistering row by the end. Landry threw her out but he knew he would have to change his plans now she was on to him. It was around then that Margaret started to look around for another person to buy Kempshott.'

Pensively, Shaw swirled the remains of the whisky round in his glass. 'Do the police know all this?' he asked.

'Yes. I went over this and Fullerton's part in it before we got called away to the fire. He got his collar felt over it and was damned lucky to get off. It rather soured the relationship he had with Landry. Most of the money I paid for Kempshott had to go on paying the debts that Landry thought Fullerton had successfully buried. DI Burrell was extremely interested.'

'I bet he was!' Shaw agreed.

Dering took one last sip of whisky. 'I'd

better get those rooms sorted out and see if we can rustle up some food for a buffet for your friends. I'll let that nice lady, Karin, put the word round.'

'It's very kind of you to go to all this trouble,' Shaw said a little awkwardly.

Dering paused, then posed Shaw a question. 'When you rescued my friends from their burning house, did you do it to be kind, or were you doing what any decent human being would try to do?' Seeing that the other was momentarily at a loss how to answer, he continued. 'I would guess it was the latter. Well, I can do something to help the ordinary decent people who have been caught up in these horrible events.' He smiled, though it was a shadow compared to his normal beam. 'I'll see you down here later, eh?'

'You will indeed,' Shaw answered and headed off to his room to strip away the grime, the smell and, if he was lucky, some of the trauma of the fire. Emerging after half an hour and wearing fresh clothes, he felt noticeably better. There was a large group of people gathered in the bar, many with bags of one kind or another. He saw St. John and Kendrick sitting with a few of the die-hard archers and decided to join them. 'Any news on Smithy or the others?' he asked.

'Some,' Kendrick answered him. 'Smithy called me just a few minutes ago from the hospital. They've said he's free to leave. No real damage done. He asked how the two women were doing and got the usual line about no kinship, no information, but you know Smithy. He'd got chatting to the paramedics in the ambulance and one of them happened to see him on their way back out of the hospital. He was told that they were stable and that the older one had started to come round.'

'Thank God for that!' Shaw felt a tension lift a little inside his chest. He was still somehow hollow inside, which he supposed was a reaction to the shock of the whole experience.

'What the hell is going on here, Nick? Do you have any idea?' Kendrick asked, frustrated. 'First we get a corpse on the field and we all think we've killed someone; then he turns out to have been dead already. Now somebody torches a house to kill two old birds. It's madness!'

Shaw shrugged helplessly. 'I don't know much more than you do, Matt.'

'Well, what about that weirdo who was hanging around the tents on Saturday morning? Do they know who he was? Leon said he might have swiped the arrows. There's also the car Will and I saw driving off just before the fire.'

Shaw's ears pricked up at this. 'What car?'

Will answered the question in his usual broad accent. 'I was lookin' at a couple o' bows Matt had fer sale when I heard a car engine a little way off. Next thing there was a red blur behind the field as someone drove off pretty sharpish. Ye don't really notice that track at the back wi' the hedges but the colour stood oot,' Hazard explained. He was looking a damn sight cleaner than the last time Shaw had seen him and had even shaved.

'Have you told the police about it?' Shaw asked.

'Aye. I collared that youngster they left on site an' got him to write it doon.'

Hazard turned to St. John. 'I'll probably stay the night. It's a long drive back up tae Ayrshire and I don't want to dae it in the dark, no' efter a day like this.'

St. John reached inside his jacket and brought out a crumpled piece of paper. 'I'm keeping a list of who wants to go home so I can ask DI Burrell what we should do. In fact,' he said, scanning the room, 'it might not be a bad idea to get a show of hands while we've got most of us here.' He quickly did so and then went off to check with anyone who had stayed at the campsite.

'He's very good at this, isn't he?' Shaw commented.

'Yes. Leon may not be the best archer you could meet but he's great on the details, the practicalities. That's why we vote him back as chairman every year, poor sod,' Kendrick answered. 'I wish Smithy would get here soon. I offered to go and pick him up but he said he'd get a taxi.'

* * *

It was in fact only a short time later that Smithy returned, just in time to get a late lunch from the buffet. Dering's staff had set a couple of long tables up in the lounge and piled them with sandwiches, sausage rolls and fruit. By then everyone had joined them up at the hotel and Smithy was greeted with a cheer. He raised his hand in appreciation. 'Thanks everyone and yes, Matt, I'll take you up on that pint you were just about to buy me.' That got a laugh.

All eyes were on Smithy but Shaw noticed a smaller figure standing behind him. It was Louisa and there were six police officers with her. She came to the centre of the room and addressed the crowd.

'Good evening, everyone. I'm afraid that we have to bother you again but hopefully this will be the last time. It's the same drill as before. We'll take a statement from each of you so if you can all stay here for now, we'll set up in the bar and get started.' She moved over to Shaw and gave him a brief, taut smile. 'I also need to get fingerprints from you and Smithy to eliminate any prints you may have left at the cottage. It was definitely arson and may yet be murder.'

5

The afternoon wore into evening. Louisa and her team painstakingly interviewed everyone who had been at the campsite and then all the staff at the hotel. Shaw poured himself a coffee from the huge urn that Stephanie had set up for police and guests alike, then took it outside. He was joined by Smithy, the big man wiping the ink off his fingers with the rag he usually used to clean his arrows.

'Well, that was a new experience. I've never been fingerprinted before,' Smithy commented wryly.

'Me neither. How are you doing?' Shaw asked.

Smithy hesitated, scratching his thick beard. 'All right, I suppose, but a bit . . . oh, I don't know.'

'How did you get back from the hospital?'

'Louisa found a place for me in the cop car. Seems she'd just dropped her boss off at the hospital.' Smithy looked anxious and after a pause blurted out: 'They don't know if she'll survive, the old woman I pulled out of the house. Louisa said she had been doing all right but then some kind of complication happened and she still might die.'

'Christ,' Shaw said quietly. He had thought that must be the kind of thing Louisa had meant earlier but it hit harder to hear it spelled out.

'I don't know what to do with myself at the moment,' Smithy admitted. 'If Trish was here that would help, but she's working this weekend.'

'There's always the option of getting drunk,' Shaw suggested half-heartedly.

Smithy shook his head. 'Believe me, I'm tempted, but it just doesn't have the usual appeal at the moment.' He sat down heavily on a section of stone wall. 'Do the police have any idea who did all this?' he asked desperately. 'Has Louisa told you anything?'

'She can't really say much, but there are some things I've heard from Dering that seem to be putting a possible suspect in the frame.'

'I've been meaning to ask — why didn't Louisa tell us she's a copper? She's been coming along with you for what, two, three years now? Ever since that red-haired girl ditched you.'

'Don't remind me.' Shaw grimaced. 'Left me and took my best longbow with her.' He glanced back to the windows of the bar. He could just make out Louisa, interviewing the last of the staff. 'When I met Louisa it took her two months to tell me she was a police officer. When I asked her why the reticence, she said that the moment people hear someone's working for the Old Bill they change, ever so slightly. A barrier goes up. She loves her job but when she's off duty she likes to be really off duty. I had to persuade her to confess all to my family and I'll admit that when she told them, there was this pause, just a small one, and I realised she was right. People get over it of course, but I could understand why she prefers to be just *Louisa* whenever she can.'

'I hadn't thought of it like that,' Smithy mused — something he rarely did. 'It's been handy, I suppose, having one of us helping the police here. I noticed that Burrell didn't ask too many stupid questions about archery, which saved some time. And don't get me wrong about Louisa; she's sound. She's doing a good job keeping it all moving.'

'Yes. She once told me that for people like her who are both nosy and bossy, it's the — '

'Perfect job.' Smithy finished the sentence for Shaw and they both laughed.

'Am I missing something, guys?' came Louisa's voice from behind them, and they spun round looking slightly guilty. She walked out across the lawn to join them. 'We've finished for the night and I hope to God that nothing else happens today.'

'Do you think we'll be able to leave in the morning? Trish called to ask if she should come down here, you know, if we have to stay much longer.'

'I can't promise anything, but I don't see any reason why we'd need to keep you.' She put her hand on Smithy's arm. 'If I were you I'd get inside. There are about twenty people ready to buy you a drink.'

'Well, maybe just a couple would be nice,' Smithy conceded and went back into the hotel looking a little less troubled than he had when he came out.

'Was anyone offering to buy me a drink?' Shaw asked. 'Just out of interest.'

Louisa hooked her arm through his. 'Plenty of people were but *I've* booked you for this evening. What would you say to a nice meal, somewhere other than here? I could really do with a break from all of this, just for a few hours.'

Shaw carefully took a stray lock of her hair and tucked it behind her ear. 'I seem to remember seeing a rather expensive dress in your suitcase. I think it deserves to be worn.'

Louisa leant her head to one side. 'That raises a point. Do *you* have anything smart to wear?'

'I always bring a full black tie outfit to archery events!' Shaw exclaimed in mock outrage, then enveloped her in his arms. 'I've got a jacket that should do, and if you walk in first wearing that dress, no one's going to give me a second glance.' He turned round to look up at the front elevation of the hotel. 'For some indefinable reason it's growing on me, this place, even given the circumstances. I thought it looked a bit stolid at first, but I think it has a good vibe. Kind of . . . dependable.' He frowned. 'I don't suppose there's any chance of you turning your phone off this evening?' he asked without much hope.

'Sorry, none at all. We might get news from the hospital,' Louisa replied regretfully.

'Oh, fair enough. Come on, you have a bath and I'll find out where we can go.'

*   *   *

By ten o'clock Shaw felt a lot more relaxed, only partly because of the wine. Mostly it was the blessed relief of being with Louisa as herself once again. He greatly respected her professionalism but it was still strange to see her at work. They had purposefully talked about normal things: their plans for painting the flat, the pros and cons of getting a cat, where to go on holiday. The soft lighting in the restaurant glinted off Louisa's shimmering dress and a few times they even forgot about Kempshott and its crimes. After they had finished eating Louisa brought the conversation round to the archery.

'I forgot to ask Leon, did they get the chance to do the prize-giving in all the commotion?'

'I hadn't thought about that,' Shaw answered. 'Not that I'm aware of. I know we didn't win anything this time.'

'Oh well, there'll be other times. Do you want a coffee, or shall we go now?'

Shaw thought about it. On the one hand he was pretty tired and the idea of falling into bed was a very pleasant one. On the other, he knew that when they set foot inside Kempshott Louisa might get waylaid by people eager for news. She looked relaxed and happy right now and he wanted that to last a little longer. 'I think a coffee would be nice,' he decided.

They moved to a leather sofa by the fireplace but had only been chatting a few minutes when Louisa's phone buzzed with a text message. She read it, then said: 'It's from DI Burrell. I'm going to have to call him.'

'Okay, I'd better pay up and then we can go.' Shaw managed not to sound disappointed. When Louisa came back into the restaurant he was ready to leave. They walked to the car and Louisa filled him in as she drove.

'Margaret Norden is fully conscious and was able to give a statement of sorts. Apparently she and Janice had been shopping. When they came home, Janice unlocked the back door and walked in a little ahead of Margaret, who had stopped for a moment to see how her flowers were doing. She thought she heard a funny noise from the cottage, just a small one, and went inside. She didn't see Janice so she went to put her handbag down in the kitchen and that's it, that's all she can remember. They're going to keep her in for the moment for observation but there's also a question mark about her leaving hospital, as returning to the cottage is completely out of the question.'

'So what do you think happened?' Shaw asked. 'Was the attacker hiding in the cottage?'

Louisa nodded. 'It seems likely, doesn't it? He could have knocked Janice out and taken her body upstairs — Smithy found her on the landing — then hit Margaret when her back was turned. According to the hospital, she's slightly deaf. They also said that she seemed to be a little confused at times, though whether that was a permanent thing or a result of the attack they couldn't say. Either way we can't take her story as gospel, even though it sounds very plausible.' She swung the car into the long driveway leading to the hotel.

'Any news on Janice?' Shaw asked a little hesitantly.

'She's in a stable condition, which doesn't mean a lot, but she hasn't come round properly. That's partly due to the medication she's on. I gather the burns on her legs are deep and will be extremely painful, so they're keeping her pretty doped up with morphine. She took quite a downturn earlier and they have to be very careful about infection. There's also the blow to the head. She's been scanned and there doesn't appear to be damage, but to be honest we'll just have to wait and see how things go.'

They got out of the car and walked to the entrance. Looking through the windows, Shaw could see there were still at least twenty of the archery group settled in the lounge and bar. He was just wondering if they could possibly sneak past everyone without a barrage of questions when Louisa gently pulled his arm.

'Let's go round this way instead,' she said, leading him to the kitchens at the back of the house. This area was far darker than the beautifully lit front of Kempshott and they stumbled a little on the uneven flagstones, but there was a light visible above the kitchen door and they made for it.

Two kitchen workers were having a cigarette by the door and after they recognised Louisa they allowed both of them to go in. Shaw couldn't help but switch into work mode, scanning the surfaces for dirt or left-out food, but the whole place was spotless stainless steel and carefully placed utensils. He would add that to his review of Kempshott — if he ever got the chance to write it, that was.

They emerged into a corridor that was obviously part of the old servants' quarters but now had lists of staff rotas pinned up on the walls. There was also a photograph which must have been taken in the 1930s. It was a group shot of Kempshott's servants, from a man who must have been the butler down to the housemaids and gardeners. They all had the slightly stilted look of people unused to being photographed. Below it had been pinned a modern take on the photograph. Shaw saw Dering had taken the butler's position, Stephanie was the housekeeper and so on. It was a nice touch and he couldn't help but smile.

Louisa was already far down the corridor and had knocked on a door. Shaw caught her up and was not surprised when Dering came out.

'Louisa! Is there any news?' he asked worriedly

'Yes. Margaret's awake and has been asking if you would go and see her in the morning,' Louisa answered.

'Thank God!' Dering said with relief.

'But what about Janice? Is she all right?'

'It's going to be a bit longer before we know that. DI Burrell wanted to thank you for the information about Janice's sister. She's been contacted and I believe is going to travel down from Dumfries tomorrow.'

'That's something at least. Why don't you come in and have a nightcap?' Dering ushered them into his office, which looked rather more like a living room. There were two old but comfortable sofas, bookcases covering most of the wall space and a wonderfully deep carpet.

Looking down, Shaw noticed that Dering had left his smart shoes by the door and was padding about in his socks.

Handing them each a glass of brandy, Dering sat on one of the sofas. 'Poor Janice. She's been such a help to Margaret this past year. She might've had to go into a home if Janice hadn't agreed to move in.'

Louisa took a sip of the brandy. 'Oh, that's the proper stuff all right!' she commented appreciatively. 'Is Janice a friend, or does she work for Margaret?'

'Both. Janice was the last housekeeper

here and helped Margaret get through the process of selling up and moving. I think she got a job somewhere else but stayed in touch, and eventually Margaret asked if Janice would be her paid live-in companion — to use Margaret's phrase. They get on very well, partly because Janice, although she's very quietly spoken, can stand up to Margaret.'

'From what we've been hearing, that's no mean task, but I'm finding it hard to think of her like that. She was so small and frail this afternoon.' Shaw remembered that she hardly weighed more than a child.

'She may be old now but it's all about strength of will with Margaret.' Dering put his glass down on a side table and reached out to the dark oak bookcase. He pulled out a slim volume entitled *Kempshott and the Percevals*. It must have dated from the 1950s, judging by the design. He flicked through the pages until he found the pictures. 'Here. This is Margaret in her twenties. She's the one with the gun.'

Louisa raised her eyebrows and took the book.

The photograph showed a young woman with a hunting rifle crooked over her arm. At her feet was an impressive array of dead pheasants, pigeons and partridges. Concentrating on Margaret Norden's face, she saw a determined set to her jaw and a look of satisfaction, presumably at a successful day's shooting.

'She was always very physical — riding, shooting, playing sports. Until a few years ago she still played golf. The slim figure she kept all that time has become rather fragile now I'm afraid, but her spirit is still there. At least I hope it still is.' Dering took the book back and carefully replaced it. 'Are you any closer to catching the man responsible for all this?' He sounded tired and slightly desperate.

'Possibly. We do have a few leads to follow up but I can't tell you anything definite yet.' She rose to her feet. 'Thank you, Mr. Dering. The brandy was sublime. I think I need an early night, but I do have a favour to ask . . .'

Dering took them to the back stairs, now an emergency exit for the hotel, and they were able to bypass all the public areas. Louisa slipped off her high heels and they quietly made their way to their room, leaving all the questions and suppositions behind for the night.

★ ★ ★

'Louisa! Louisa!' Shaw sleepily nudged her. 'Your phone just buzzed. Might be important.'

It was a little after seven in the morning and Louisa was dead to the world.

Shaw leaned over her to reach the mobile. He fumbled his way to the message and read it blearily. Then he sat up properly and threw the covers off. Shaking Louisa awake, he said: 'Burrell wants you to go to the hospital by eight-thirty. Janice is awake and talking!'

By a quarter past eight, Shaw had driven them both to the hospital and they were waiting outside the ward for Janice to be ready to see Louisa. Shaw was itching to see how she was and to hear anything she could tell them, but he knew Louisa couldn't invite him. He contented himself with feeling relieved that Janice had regained consciousness and hoping that he would be able to report good news back to Smithy.

'You can go in now,' the staff nurse finally told Louisa. 'The morphine will make her drowsy but it's very necessary at the moment. If you feel she's fading or in distress I'll be just round the corner.'

Louisa left and Shaw settled down to think. An idea had been forming at the back of his mind for a while and he now had the leisure to consider it properly. It was his turn to play the detective. Presumably the murder and the attempted murders were linked and were, at least to some extent, planned in advance. The placing of John Fullerton's body was not coincidental. The blind shoot had been used to try to cover up the gunshot wound with arrow damage. But how exactly did the arrows get into Fullerton? Had the murderer got a bow from somewhere and shot him at close range? Maybe he had just stabbed them in, but that, whilst not impossible, would have taken quite a lot of force. There was also the question of why Fullerton had been on that track at the back of the fields to begin with. Was he meeting someone?

Moving on to the cottage attack — could it have been an interrupted robbery? Janice might have come in and found a thief, let out a cry and then been silenced. The thief had then lain in wait for Margaret. But it didn't really make sense for a casual thief to set fire to the cottage and risk being charged with murder, rather than just running off. However, if the intruder had been recognised by the women and could be identified, that changed things, he supposed. On the whole though, he was pretty convinced that it had always been a calculated intention to kill.

Shaw looked at his watch, wondering how long Louisa would be. He didn't feel comfortable in hospitals, and never had, certain that they had a particular smell not found anywhere else. He got to his feet, abandoning the rather uncomfortable chair in favour of a wander along the corridor perusing the usual depressing and somewhat alarmist posters. All the exhortations to look out for signs of illness were well-meant, he supposed, but seemed to him to promote worry rather than well-being.

By the time Louisa returned, he had decided he probably had three serious diseases. Finding him staring worriedly at the list of symptoms for diabetes, she tugged his arm and said: 'Stop window shopping, Nick. You can't afford it.'

Shaw gave an apologetic grimace. 'How'd it go with Janice? Is she okay?'

Louisa looked pensive and considered her answer before speaking. 'Okay may be pushing it. I'm sure that she's going to have emotional repercussions from this and the nurse said that the burns will need a lot of treatment to heal properly. She'll certainly need a skin graft.' They started walking down the corridor. 'You can let Smithy know that she's out of danger and is expected to make a good recovery, but it's going to take a long time.'

'Did she see anything of her attacker?' Shaw asked curiously.

'Yes and no. The cottage was locked as usual when they came back from the shops and Janice went in first with her bags. She put them down on a table and then someone hit her on the back of the head. She fell forward but didn't immediately black out. She looked up from the floor and saw a figure in a mask. 'Something hairy that you might get at Halloween' were her words. Although she couldn't make out the face, she says that amid the shock, she had a sense of familiarity — that the attacker was not a stranger. She couldn't remember anything from that point up to waking up in hospital.'

'So she couldn't give you a name?' Shaw asked, with a feeling of disappointment.

Louisa shook her head. 'Not unless there's something else that she remembers later. The attacker was very careful, wearing a mask and, Janice thinks, gloves too. I think the forensic team will be allowed to examine the cottage today. The view of the fire crew was that it has probably collapsed as much as it's going to. They might find something but I'm not all that hopeful.'

They reached the end of the corridor

and pushed open the double doors.

'Excuse me! Officer!' The shout came from behind them and they turned to see the staff nurse running towards them.

'What's wrong?' Louisa asked sharply, and Shaw could see that she had tensed up.

'Miss Mudie's calling for you. She's quite insistent,' the nurse explained breathlessly.

They hastened back to the small room, where Janice Mudie was in a state of agitation. Shaw stopped at the door but he could see her well enough. Janice was sitting up in bed, looking frail and anguished. It seemed as if there was a mound of blankets on the bed but Shaw belatedly realised the covers were actually supported by a kind of frame over her legs to keep the burns free of pressure.

'Thank God you're still here,' Janice sobbed, clasping Louisa's hand. 'It's come back to me.' She paused, obviously trying to find enough composure to speak clearly.

'Take your time, Janice. It's all right,' Louisa reassured the frightened woman.

On her face was an expression of calm sympathy. Janice took some deep, shuddering breaths.

The nurse leaned over her from the other side of the bed. 'Do you need some more morphine?'

'No!' Janice answered with force, then added a little more quietly: 'I can't fall asleep yet. I have to say this.' She turned her head towards Louisa again. 'I remembered falling over and looking up at him, like I told you, and I couldn't see his face because of the mask. But I just realised that I saw something when he raised his arm to hit me again. The sleeve of his coat rode up and there was a copper bracelet, the kind that has magnets in it to help with rheumatism, you know? Well I've seen that before, that exact one.' She spoke with emphasis, staring at Louisa intently. 'There was a deep scratch on it and I know who owns it.' Janice paused and seemed to be gathering her strength. Then she burst out: 'It's that bastard, Michael Landry!'

6

Standing outside the hospital, Louisa had called Burrell. Janice had remained adamant that although she hadn't seen his face, her attacker *was* Michael Landry — one-time owner of Kempshott. Finishing the call, Louisa turned back to Shaw. 'Drop me off at the station, Nick. We need to follow this up immediately.'

'Landry's name had been rolling about in the back of my mind since Dering mentioned him,' Shaw said as they walked through the huge hospital car park. As with most hospitals these days there were drivers circling, waiting for someone to leave in order to grab the space.

'You're not the only one. I know that the DI asked for Landry's last known address yesterday. If Janice is right, he must be at least a little crazy. I mean, the only thing he would have to gain from his actions is revenge.'

'Aren't all murderers a little crazy?' Shaw objected.

Louisa shook her head. 'No, not at all. Many have perfectly sane reasons, usually monetary gain, for killing. They just don't let normal morals hold them back.'

They had reached the car and Shaw looked in dismay at the sliver of space between the driver's door and the next car.

Louisa's mouth twitched as she saw the problem. Her side was just about okay for her to slide through but there was no way Shaw would manage. She opened the car boot saying: 'It's lucky we've got an estate car. Go on, climb through.'

Shaw sighed and awkwardly clambered over the seats, thankful that at least the bows were back at the hotel. Finally and very carefully, he reversed out of the space. A small blue car was lying in wait and he saw the driver wave to him. Recognising Dering, who must be on his way to visit Margaret and Janice, he muttered to Louisa: 'Can we say anything to him about Landry?'

'Better not for now. I need to check it

with the DI first.'

Shaw nodded slightly and then wound down his window. 'If you can get in here you're welcome to the space.'

'I've never seen a car do a better impression of a sardine,' Dering called back. 'I should be okay. Bearing in mind what this place is like, I borrowed Stephanie's little motor. Louisa, are you going to give the go-ahead for all the archery folk to leave today? They're getting a bit anxious.'

Louisa leant across Shaw to answer. 'I'll get a message out as soon as I can, believe me.'

'If you could. Apart from anything else, I know that the portaloos are due to be taken away at noon.'

'I'll bear that in mind,' she answered and they drove off.

'Now there's a man who doesn't lose track of the practicalities!' Shaw chuckled.

They left the boundaries of the hospital and headed for the centre of town, Louisa directing their way through the road system.

It didn't take them long to reach the police station, during which time Shaw wondered what his next move should be. Pulling into the large courtyard at the back of the station, he addressed the problem. 'Louisa, what's going to happen next?' he asked.

'I report what Janice has alleged to Burrell and we investigate further. I fully expect that he will give the okay to dismiss everyone as we haven't found a single connection between the tournament and the attacks.'

'I mean, what should *I* do? I can stay on at Kempshott for a bit but I'll need to be back home by Wednesday. I didn't think to bring my laptop along this weekend.'

'Oh, I'm sorry. I hadn't thought about that.' She paused and thought it over for a moment. 'To be honest I've no idea how much longer I'll be here. It was convenient for Burrell to bring me in to begin with but I can't stay on indefinitely. I know DI Mercer won't countenance that.'

Shaw nodded in agreement. Louisa's immediate boss, Frank Mercer, would want her back as soon as possible.

'I'll ask Burrell about it today and also see if there's somewhere more appropriate for me to stay. I don't somehow think the force would foot the bill for an extended holiday at a country house hotel.' She turned more to face Shaw. 'I know you can't just hang around while I do my job. This was only supposed to be a quick weekend away.'

'Yeah. I've really got to get my head down soon on some work for the new guidebook for Bath.' Shaw looked out of his window at the 1960s building that housed this branch of the Hampshire Constabulary. 'Off you go then. Find out what you can and we'll take it from there. I'm going to explore Basingstoke for a bit but I should be back at Kempshott by lunchtime if you want to get hold of me.'

Louisa gave him an exasperated look. 'Just keep your mobile on for a change. It won't hurt you!' She kissed him goodbye and got out.

Shaw watched her take the steps to the glass doors at a jog. As a man who shunned most forms of exercise, he sometimes envied

Louisa her energetic approach to life. The one thing he did do a lot of was walking. It was how he had got into travel writing in the first place. His students' union had wanted to produce a guide for freshers, showing them Bristol from a student's perspective. Having wanted to try his hand at journalism, he had volunteered to compile the booklet and ended up an authority on the city. The hours spent traversing Bristol by bus and on foot had been some of his best times at university and he still enjoyed exploring new places. Louisa had once remarked that he'd unwittingly mastered the policeman's walk.

He parked the car in the city centre and set off in a random direction. The simple act of walking had its usual uplifting effect and he spent a pleasant hour wandering round the back streets of Basingstoke. He was leaving the grounds of a medium-sized park when he noticed a familiar figure leaning against the bandstand some way ahead of him. Shaw continued cautiously along the path, trying to work out where he had seen the man before. He was about fifty and slightly unkempt, with short brown curly hair. He racked his brain, trying to put a context to the feeling of recognition. The man shifted his weight slightly. He appeared to be either waiting or killing time. Then it came to him — this was the man he had seen hanging around the campsite on the first day's shooting.

Shaw slowed his pace, thinking frantically. The man might have nothing to do with the corpse — or everything. Should he try to talk to him, call the police, attempt a citizen's arrest? He sat down on the nearest bench, keeping the man in sight. Well, he could rule out the last option as the man was doing nothing wrong, so he couldn't arrest him. He felt uncomfortable about approaching him overtly, so that left calling the police — or more precisely, calling Louisa. He called her mobile.

'Hi, Nick. What's up?'

'I need advice.' Shaw briefly and quietly appraised her of his quandary.

'Are you certain it's him? We only saw the man by the gate for a minute or two.'

'Yes. I noticed at the time there was a

tear in the pocket of his Barbour coat. This guy matches exactly. What should I do?' He tried not to sound too anxious.

'We'll be there in . . . ' She broke off to ask a colleague. 'In less than ten minutes. If he leaves, try to follow him but don't do anything stupid. He's an unknown quantity at this stage. If you have to move, call me.'

Shaw slid the mobile back into his pocket and hoped fervently that his quarry wouldn't go anywhere. As the minutes passed it looked like he was in luck. The Lurker, as Shaw had mentally christened him, remained in place, leaning furtively against one of the uprights of the bandstand. He didn't seem to have noticed his observer at all. Eight minutes after Louisa had rung off, the Lurker took one last look across the fresh green lawns and started walking away.

Shaw cursed under his breath and waited another thirty seconds before following. If Louisa got here as quickly as she had hoped, they might meet the police car as they exited the park, but what if the traffic had been bad? Or what if this guy was completely innocent and thought he was being stalked? A lot would depend on how he reacted when confronted by the police.

The Lurker reached the exit and turned to the right.

Shaw hung back. He could see a long way up the street and could keep an eye on the man without crowding him. Looking up and down he could see no sign of a police car, marked or otherwise, and he was getting impatient. Surely they should be here now? He started to walk up the street with the Lurker far ahead, trying to use his mobile as he walked. Looking back up after dialling Louisa's number, he was startled to see there was no sign of the man. He broke into a run. There was only one side street ahead and he darted round the corner into it. At the far end of that street he saw his quarry turn quickly to the right. Louisa's voice sounded in his ear.

'Where are you?'

'Two right turns away from the exit. I can't see a street name yet. He must have seen me and took off.'

'Can you still see him?' Louisa asked

tensely. 'We're only a couple of streets away.'

Shaw pounded along the pavement, hindered somewhat by the awkwardness of running with one hand, holding the phone up to his ear. He reached the corner and was relieved to see that the man he was shadowing had slowed down. There was also a street sign. 'We're on Rectory Avenue!'

'Got it!' Louisa sounded triumphant. 'Hang in there, Nick. We're nearly with you.'

'Okay!' he panted. The Lurker was doggedly jogging along the avenue ahead of him and he allowed himself to ease up a little. He suddenly had the urge to play the fool. To do something like shout out to the man: 'I'm only after a light!' or 'Did you know you dropped your wallet?' Fortunately for him, a police car appeared at the end of the avenue and Louisa got out of the passenger seat.

'Excuse me, sir!' she said in an authoritative voice. 'We'd just like to ask you a few questions.

The stranger sank onto the low wall of a garden, looking defeated. He jerked his thumb towards Shaw, who was walking up to meet them. 'Is he with you then?' he gasped.

'Yes,' Louisa confirmed.

'Why the hell didn't you say so then?' He turned accusingly to Shaw. Without waiting for an answer, he reached into his jacket pocket and took out his wallet. Extracting a card, he handed it to Louisa.

She read it aloud, her eyebrows raised: 'George Peterson. Private Investigator.'

★   ★   ★

It had turned into a warm day, with blue skies overhead and fresh green grass underfoot. It felt like summer was just round the corner. Picking his way round the few remaining guy ropes at the campsite, Shaw welcomed the heat. He was bagging up litter — not that there was a lot of it, but some had inevitably accumulated over the course of the weekend and as they had all been obliged to spend an extra night, there was a little more than usual. Only a handful of people were still there, the ones who lived not far away. He had helped Smithy pack the last of his stuff and was able to reassure him that Janice was on the mend.

As Smithy was about to drive off, he leaned out of the window and asked Shaw a question: 'Nick, if the police catch the murderer, will you get to know about it? Through Louisa, I mean?'

'I'd think so. Even if she has to leave the case she'd be able to ask how it panned out.'

'Would you let me know what happens? I'd really like to know who's been behind all this.' Smithy looked out at the view. From here they could see the campsite with the wood behind it and rising slightly above all, Kempshott House. It looked beautiful in the sunshine, with light glinting off the many windows. 'It's a cracking place and I'd like to come back but it's going to take a while to get that fire out of my head.'

Shaw nodded in agreement. 'You and me both, Smithy. Well, safe journey home. I'll be in touch as and when there's an arrest or whatever.'

Smithy had left, arm raised for a moment out of the window.

It was true about the fire, Shaw thought. Everything about it seemed to be embedded in his memory so vividly. Shutting his eyes for a moment, he could recall exactly what he had experienced — the horribly thick air, the smell of burning hurting his nostrils and lungs, and the ferocious heat itself. The fire couldn't have been burning for long but even then the heat had been intense. He shuddered involuntarily and opened his eyes. The calming scene of bucolic serenity helped to restore his equilibrium, but he decided at that moment to leave Kempshott in the morning.

'Nick! Can I have a hand, mate?' It was Kendrick, labouring under the weight of no less than five bows. Shaw loped over and extricated three of them, being careful not to tangle the strings.

'I didn't know you brought this many bows, Matt. Couldn't bear to leave any behind?' Shaw joked.

'Yeah, right. Actually, only two are mine. The yew bow you're holding and this nice bamboo one here.' He tapped the side of an attractive black bow with the tell-tale ridges.

They carried the bows to Kendrick's car and slid the first two in over the back seats to rest just behind the handbrake.

'This one is Leon's and so is the quiver. I'm dropping it off at his place while he finishes up here. The smaller one in your right hand is a lemonwood and walnut one that I said I'd take down a bit for someone who wants to give it to their son.' Kendrick slammed the boot and turned round holding the final bow. 'And this . . . is a mystery. Karin and Lars found it when they packed up the last of their stuff. You know they always come with loads of garden furniture? Well this was underneath the zip-up bag they keep the cushions in.'

Shaw automatically reached for the bow. Once you had got the archery bug, another person's bow was always interesting; the feel, the weight, the balance — all bows were unique. However, Kendrick held it back out of reach. 'Down, boy!' he remonstrated. 'You don't want to get even more fingerprints on this, do you? I've got gloves on but you haven't.' Seeing Shaw's expression of dawning comprehension, he continued: 'I've never been to a shoot where someone has forgotten to take their bow home with them. Not in fifteen years. Now I know it's been a damn strange time for everyone, but even so . . .'

'You think it might be linked to the murder?' Shaw asked with growing excitement.

'Possibly. Although I don't know if it could've actually shot those arrows.' Kendrick pointed to the upper buffalo horn nock, the tip of the bow that had a groove for the string to lie in. 'You see this? It's been damaged at some point — look.' He gently wiggled the nock, demonstrating its very loose hold on the bow. 'It you try to shoot that bow the nock's not going to take the strain.'

Shaw remembered Louisa saying that the arrows may have been stuck into the victim by hand. 'Christ, you could be right! Have you told the police yet?'

'It was only a short time ago that I put two and two together. I was going to put a message on the Facebook site to say 'bow found' or something but then I thought about it a bit more and, well, it might be important.'

'Have you got a number for the investigation?' Shaw asked.

Kendrick looked surprised. 'Can't we just call Louisa?'

'I'm pretty sure she's unavailable right now,' Shaw answered. Certainly when he had left her they were taking Peterson, the Private Investigator, back to the station to 'answer a few questions'. He had been dying to hear what the man had to say but would have to wait.

'Oh, all right then. I suppose I can take it round to the police on my way home. I'll be leaving as soon as I've got the last bits and pieces in the car.'

Shaw explained where the station was and then wandered back to the edge of the campsite. St. John was helping the last stragglers to pack up and soon there would be no sign that they had ever been there. He walked a little further, following the path he had taken to the cottage the day before. As he got nearer the faint smell of smoke that was lingering grew stronger. Even with all the water that had been pumped onto it the smell was there. He had to stop outside the garden, as the police's striped tape had been wound round the trees that surrounded the clearing. The effect was bizarrely decorative. It must have been a lovely home once, he thought. A pretty, old-fashioned cottage with a garden that faded gently into the surrounding wood with no fence to mar the look. Of course, that had also meant that it had been easy for the arsonist to get in.

It was obvious that the cottage would not be salvageable. There was precious little left of it. Shaw wondered where Margaret and Janice would live, both for the interim and in the long term. By the sound of her, Margaret wouldn't want to go anywhere but Kempshott. He made a mental note to ask Louisa if any plans had been made. With one last look at the pitiful blackened shell of the cottage, he returned to the hotel.

★   ★   ★

Having decided to head home the next day, Shaw wanted to spend the afternoon working on his piece about Kempshott. He ordered a large pot of tea and chose a chair with a table — probably a card table, he guessed — in the lounge to work at. This time the words flowed properly and he found he could write a sensible review, covering all the usual aspects and omitting any mention of murder and arson. His tea had arrived on a warming tray and had stayed beautifully hot — another of Dering's nice touches. In fact, Shaw found that he was having to rein himself in a little. No one would believe the review if he was too fulsome about the delights of the hotel. Trying to think of a negative, he decided on the direct approach. He had done this on occasions before and it generally proved useful.

Stephanie was back behind the desk today, preparing invoices by the look of it. 'Stephanie, can I ask you a few questions?' Shaw asked as he reached the desk.

She looked up with a smile and held up one manicured finger for a moment.

Writing a few figures down on her notebook, she shuffled the papers back together. 'Sorry, I just needed to finish that last calculation or I'd have had to do the whole lot again.' She waved her hand dismissively at the laptop. 'We're having a bit of trouble with the electrics this morning. They keep going off.'

'I haven't noticed anything.' Shaw was surprised. The lights had seemed to be constant to him.

'It's only affecting the sockets and it's only brief, but it's enough to knock the computer out so I'm doing these by hand.' She pulled a spare chair over to her side of the desk. 'Come and sit down and ask me anything you want, and then I can ask you something.'

'Okay. The obvious things first: if I wanted to catch a bus into Basingstoke, how would I go about it?'

Stephanie reached for a timetable and showed him that the buses stopped about two hundred yards from the hotel and were fairly regular. She also had a map of Basingstoke with the return stop marked in. 'We keep a stock of these but most of our guests come by car.'

'That's fine. How about if I run out of something — toothpaste or shaving foam, that kind of thing? Would you be able to help me with that?'

Stephanie grinned. 'I hope I get a good grade at the end of this. We have a small supply of the most common toiletries which are available any time the front desk is open. For more unusual items we can either direct you to the village shop or, if you were unable to get there yourself, we can usually spare a member of staff to get them on your behalf and charge it to your bill.' She laughed for a moment. 'Last month we had a guest who was just desperate for a rather intimate item which I can't possibly divulge. On that occasion I'm afraid we failed to deliver. With the best will in the world we can't think of everything.'

'The mind boggles,' Shaw agreed. He ran through a few more questions of that type, all of which Stephanie was able to answer easily. Then he came to his secret weapon. 'Now I want you to tell me what is wrong with the hotel.'

For the first time her smile faltered. 'I'm sorry, what exactly do you mean?'

'Everywhere has a failing, believe me. I've been doing this job for a long time and nowhere is perfect. If you were in charge and had unlimited resources, what would you change or improve?'

Stephanie looked pensive and sat back in her chair to consider. 'Well . . . if I had the money I'd like us to have a stable with horses for hire. There's some lovely rides around here but it's difficult to find a horse. And if I'm honest, I think that the place is a little unsure of what it wants to be.' She paused for a moment, thinking how best to explain. 'My uncle has a real feeling for the history of the building and I love the redesign, but he's still finding his feet over the clientele. Are we aiming for the very top end of the market, which these days means new money, or are we catering to those who long for a bit of old-fashioned class, like Margaret? We've only been open for ten months so there's time to decide.'

'So where did the archery weekend fit in?' Shaw asked curiously.

'Brendan's keen to try lots of different things and this opportunity came up so he went for it. If it hadn't been for the trouble, I think it would have all gone smoothly.' There was a faint clicking sound and the small desk lamp briefly flickered off and on again. 'You see what I mean?' Stephanie said exasperatedly. 'We'll add that to the list: mysterious electrics!'

'Well it doesn't seem to be making too big an impact so far,' Shaw consoled her. 'You said you had something to ask me?'

'Yes, two things actually.' The smile left her face entirely and for the first time Shaw saw a flash of fear and anger behind the calm, competent, professional persona. 'Brendan wouldn't confirm it to me but I heard a rumour that Michael Landry might be mixed up in the attack on Margaret and Janice. Is it true?'

Shaw wavered. He didn't know how much he could say yet. 'I'm not sure. I suppose it's a possibility.'

Her jaw set determinedly and she nodded briefly. 'Margaret told me about him several times. He's a weasel. The trouble she had getting him out of here. Do you want to see what he looks like?' she asked suddenly.

'Okay, if you've got a picture.'

Stephanie pulled open a drawer and rummaged in it for a moment or two. 'Here it is,' she announced, pulling out an old brochure. Turning it over, she showed Shaw the photograph on the back of a smiling couple standing outside the entrance of the hotel. Shaw guessed they were in their fifties and looked prosperous, if a little smug. Michael Landry was clean-shaven and had short grey hair. His suit was unremarkable but Shaw's eyes were immediately drawn to the glint of metal at one of the cuffs. Looking closely, he could just make out a copper bracelet on the man's wrist.

'He came round here once, when we were refurbishing the hotel. He tried to make out that he still owned the furniture and we had no entitlement to it.' Stephanie had a steely-eyed look as she spoke. 'He brought out an official-looking document and wanted to take it all away in a lorry. Brendan told him exactly where to go with his forged paperwork and he eventually had to leave, but you could see he was the type to chance his luck at anything.'

'Well, if he is involved the police will get him, don't worry.'

'They'd better,' she said with quiet emphasis. Sliding the brochure back into the drawer, she turned back to Shaw and tried to regain her usual sunny exterior. 'I have your bill up to date so far and I was wondering if you were staying with us for longer?'

'Unless something comes up I think we'll be leaving tomorrow,' Shaw replied apologetically.

'No problem. But if you change your mind we do have room.' She smiled properly this time. 'There was one more thing you could help me with . . . '

'Anything!' Shaw answered expansively, responding to the warmth of that smile.

'I was hoping for a phone number for Will, Will Hazard?' she answered with a twinkle in her eye that reminded him of her uncle.

'I could get that for you. Has he left

something behind?' Shaw asked, rather confusedly.

'No, he offered to teach me archery and I had some *private* lessons in mind,' she answered with a look of pure mischief.

Shaw felt his eyes widen. The idea of Hazard being attractive had never intruded on his thoughts, particularly to a beautiful and sophisticated woman like Stephanie. Seeing his reaction, she laughed. 'Sorry, I couldn't resist it. Actually, Uncle Brendan got talking to Will and they want to set up a fishing trip in Scotland sometime.'

'Now that I *can* believe,' Shaw said with a sigh of relief.

7

'I've told you a hundred times, I can walk by myself!' The voice was croaky but the will behind it was unmistakeably strong. 'I refused to be taken home by ambulance and I refuse to be mollycoddled now.'

Shaw had been adding the finishing touches to his review but his curiosity got the better of him and he strolled out of the lounge into the large entrance hall.

Margaret Norton was hobbling in, leaning heavily on a walking stick but flapping away Dering's attempts to help her. 'Stephanie, my dear! Tell your uncle that all I need is my old armchair in the drawing room and a large gin.'

'Margaret, I'm so glad to see you,' Stephanie replied, coming round the desk to give the old lady a hug. 'You're staying with us of course,' she said, as a statement not a question.

'There's nowhere else I would even consider going to while my poor house is sorted out. Janice can join us when she's well enough.' Margaret turned her attention to Dering once more. 'Where's that drink got to then, Brendan?' she demanded.

'Coming right up, Margaret,' he replied with a wink to Shaw. 'You get settled into your chair; there's someone you should meet.'

Stephanie looped Margaret's arm through her own and walked her slowly into the lounge, where Shaw was working. It was done seamlessly and Shaw was fairly sure that the old lady hadn't even noticed she was leaning rather heavily on Stephanie. Seeing them making for a rather large, old-fashioned chair near one of the windows, he nipped in front to turn the chair round.

'Yes, that's the one. Thank you, Nick,' Stephanie said as she helped Margaret lower herself into the chair. Dering brought in a gin and tonic and moved one of the small tables into place to rest it on.

'Margaret, this gentleman, Mr Shaw, is the one who saved your life. He raised the alarm and got you out of the cottage in time,' Dering said, gesturing to Shaw, who found himself fixed by a pair of dark brown eyes that seemed to see right into him.

'I'm so very glad that you both survived,' Shaw said, feeling a little embarrassed.

'Well that makes two of us!' Margaret answered. She reached out to take his hand. 'I can't possibly tell you how grateful I am, for my own sake and on behalf of Janice. We owe you a great debt.' She smiled. There was a warmth and a slight hint of mischief along with the strength of will. Releasing Shaw's hand, she sat back in the chair with a satisfied sigh. 'I think I should start by buying you a drink. What would you like, Mr. Shaw?'

'It's Nick, and I'll join you in a gin and tonic if you're offering.'

Dering brought another three drinks but Stephanie said she had to go back to the desk. 'I'll have yours then,' Dering said. 'I could do with it after these last few days.' He pulled another chair round so that the three of them formed a small semi-circle around the window.

'I'm a little surprised to see that you've been discharged from hospital. I'd heard you would be kept in for observation for a few days,' Shaw said.

'They weren't very happy to let me go actually, but I convinced them I was quite safe to be sent home,' Margaret replied.

'Ha! You bullied them, Margaret, don't deny it.' Dering snorted with amusement. 'From the moment I arrived at the hospital this morning and said we had space for her here, she was determined to leave.'

'Well there was absolutely no reason for me to stay there, taking up a bed. I know how stretched the hospitals are these days.'

'I think they could have managed for a day or two, you know. Anyway, you know you're always welcome here. Number eight is free and it's just by the lift. When you're a bit fitter we can work out what's to be done about the cottage.'

Shaw noticed that Margaret's face drooped a little at the mention of her home. What must it feel like to have lost all of that?

'Just how badly damaged is it, Brendan? Can we repair it or is it going to be a complete re-build?' she asked.

Dering ran his hand over his chin. 'To be honest, from what I've seen it's going to have to come down. All the upper storey has been obliterated and a large part of the ground floor too. The footings should be all right to build on again, if you wanted to keep the same layout.'

Shaw was wondering whether the two women would want to live there again anyway after all that had happened. He'd certainly have second thoughts about it.

'Brendan, could you come to the telephone?' Stephanie called out from the desk. She sounded worried.

'Of course,' Dering replied, walking briskly into the entrance hall.

Margaret started asking Shaw about himself and they were discussing a hotel that both had visited when Dering returned looking pale, with Stephanie following. Margaret took one look at him and blurted out: 'Oh God, it's Janice, isn't it? Is she all right?'

'No, it's nothing to do with Janice,' Dering quickly reassured her. He sat down heavily in his chair and seemed to be unable to begin explaining.

'Well, who was on the telephone then?' Margaret demanded impatiently, looking first at Stephanie, then at Dering.

'Detective Inspector Burrell.' Dering took a deep breath. 'He called to warn us. A couple of policemen will be arriving shortly, for protection.'

Shaw narrowed his eyes. 'Protection?' he asked, though he had a fair idea what it might mean.

'Apparently Louisa and Burrell interviewed a private investigator this morning and the information he gave them leads them to believe that there could be further attempts on our lives — yours, Margaret, as well as mine and even Stephanie's.' Dering looked dreadful and Stephanie only slightly better.

Shaw took in the three stunned people and stood up. 'Have you locked the doors?'

'Uh, no. I mean . . . should we, with the police on the way?' Dering ran his hand through his hair, messing up his normally neat appearance.

'They can knock. Come on, Stephanie — if there's danger then I think you ought to minimise it. Get all the keys and I'll help you. We can tell the other staff on the way.'

'I should have thought of that. Oh, Christ! What if Landry's already in here somewhere?' Dering agonised.

'Landry? Michael Landry?' Margaret sat up in her chair with a start. 'Was it him? Did he do all this?'

'The police think it's likely. Burrell is coming round himself shortly to explain. Nick, I think your idea's a good one. Stephanie, you take him with you round the building,' said Dering.

'Let's get on with it then. Are you two going to be all right here?' Stephanie asked anxiously.

Margaret flapped her hands at them. 'Off you go. We'll be fine.'

With a last glance at the two of them, Shaw and Stephanie rushed off. They recruited the kitchen staff first of all, Stephanie quickly informing the chef and his two assistants of the situation.

'Bloody hell, is this for real?' exclaimed the shaven-headed Polish chef, his hands streaked with blood from a bowl of something that looked truly awful.

'I'm afraid so, Nico. Can you lock up here and do a sweep of this side of the ground floor?'

'No problem, Steffi. The chicken livers can wait.' Nico pushed the bowl to one side and picked up a vicious-looking cleaver. 'You join Mr. Dering in the lounge,' he directed the two scared assistants.

Shaw found his heart was racing as they locked yet another door. He'd wondered whether they were doing the right thing, but the thought of just sitting around waiting for the police to arrive when at any second Landry could appear was worse than taking the risk of confronting him. 'Do you really think Landry's capable of murder?' he asked Stephanie, who was bolting the side door to the gardens.

She straightened up and led them to the last area for checking — Dering's office. 'Of all the people I've known, he's the only one I could even partially believe capable of it. I started working here a little after the main negotiations were done, but I know that he twisted and lied at every point, trying to squeeze as much money out of Brendan as he could. I also know that Margaret was determined to get him out of Kempshott and I'm pretty sure that she threatened him with the police. It's quite possible that she was going to reveal the extent of his fraud if he didn't sell up.' The office was clear so they headed back to the lounge. 'Whether that amounts to motivation for these attacks . . . And I still don't know where John Fullerton fits into this. I guess that's for the police to discover.'

Coming through the entrance hall, they saw two cars draw up. One was an ordinary car driven by Burrell, with Louisa at his side. The other was a police car with two uniformed officers.

'Well, that's a sight to make the heart leap,' Stephanie commented, unlocking the front door to allow them in.

'Thank you, Miss Dering. These are Constables Harlen and Gibson. I'd like them to stay on site for a time. Would you be able to show them over the hotel?' said Burrell.

'Here we go again,' Stephanie said quietly to Shaw with a wry smile.

'Certainly — follow me.' She led the policemen away.

'Hi, Nick. You all got the message then?' Louisa said, glancing at the gathered staff waiting in the lounge. There were a few confused-looking guests as well, none of whom Shaw recognised.

'Yes, about twenty minutes ago. What happened with that private eye bloke? Was he mixed up in this? And what's the deal with Landry? I thought you'd have at least brought him in for questioning.'

'The DI's going to talk with Dering and Margaret in a moment. I think you can be present too.' Louisa looked both tired and excited. 'A lot's happened today, and it's only three o'clock.'

Burrell was speaking. 'Thank you all for your time. I can confirm that we are currently in pursuit of a potentially dangerous suspect who might be somewhere in the hotel grounds.'

A murmur of dismay rose from the guests who had been unaware of the weekend's events, having only arrived that morning. The staff merely looked grim.

'I've installed two officers here and in a

148

short time we'll be bringing in more people to do a full sweep of the grounds. I'd ask that you all remain in the hotel's public rooms for the time being and I do assure you that I will keep you updated.' Burrell looked at Dering and Margaret. 'Could I have a word with you, please?'

Dering helped Margaret to her feet. 'I'll be with you in a minute, Inspector,' Margaret replied, 'as soon as I can get these stupid legs working properly.'

After a nudge from Louisa, Shaw went round to take the old lady's other arm and he and Dering supported her as far as the front desk.

'Is this all right, Inspector? I don't think I'll get much further,' Margaret said, sinking into the office chair recently vacated by Stephanie. 'Oh, this chair's comfy. I might have to get one of these.'

Burrell looked at the open entrance hall, all windows and light, with pursed lips. 'I'd prefer to be somewhere a little more private actually. You have an office through here, I believe?' he asked Dering.

'Yes, just down the corridor. Don't worry, Margaret — that chair has wheels.'

So saying, he took a firm hold of the back of her chair and carefully dragged it along the wooden floor to the door of his office. Looking doubtfully at the luxurious carpet, he said: 'I think we'll have to leave the chair here.'

'Oh well, give me your arm.' Margaret stoically heaved herself up and tottered to the nearest sofa. 'I may need a winch to get up again, but it's comfortable enough for now.'

'Thank you for being so accommodating,' Burrell said, taking a seat opposite her.

The others found places around the cosy room. Shaw noticed that the only window was small and looked out over the kitchen courtyard.

'This morning, with the assistance of Mr. Shaw, we had the opportunity to talk with a Mr. George Peterson. Mr. Peterson is a private investigator and the information he was able to give us has advanced the investigation considerably.' Burrell stopped as there was a knock on the door. One of the constables came in with Stephanie.

'We've checked the building, sir, and there's no sign of anyone being here who shouldn't be.'

'Good. I'd like you and Harlen to wait in the entrance hall. When the others arrive I want someone at every entrance and at least one person outside.'

'My God! Is that really necessary?' Dering exclaimed, truly shocked.

'Hopefully not, but I'm not taking any chances,' Burrell replied. 'Let me explain. Peterson was employed by the wife of John Fullerton as she was suspicious that he might be having an affair. Apparently there were too many meetings that took him away overnight, strange phone calls and the like. Peterson had been shadowing Fullerton for a week, gathering evidence, and he was firmly convinced that Mrs. Fullerton was correct. When Peterson was seen at the archery he had been following Fullerton. He had lost him on the way to Kempshott and so was not on the track behind the fields when Fullerton was killed. As he knew that Fullerton used to have a connection to Kempshott, he thought it was worth having a look around here, but he never found him. The first thing he knew about the murder was when Fullerton's name was released on Sunday. He should of course have come straight to the police, but as we've had complaints about his methods of investigation in the past he was a little reluctant.' He looked at Shaw, who was leaning against Dering's desk. 'If you hadn't spotted him I very much doubt if he would ever have come forward. It was a real stroke of luck. Once we had Peterson in the station he named the person Fullerton had been seeing. It was Elaine Landry.'

'Elaine!' Margaret looked astonished. 'Well you do surprise me. I thought she and Michael were perfectly, horribly matched.'

'It seems that something changed.' Burrell let out a deep breath. 'We'd tried to contact the Landrys as soon as Fullerton was identified — finding him at Kempshott suggested some kind of connection, so it was an obvious step. There had been no reply to phone calls or to an officer calling at their house. After we received Peterson's information, Detective

152

Sergeant West and I went to the house again and after we got no response, we checked round all the windows to see if anyone was trying to avoid us. When we went round to the back of the house we saw a body lying on the floor of the conservatory. It was Elaine Landry — she'd been shot.'

There was a gasp from all those in the room except for Burrell and Louisa. Shaw felt almost numb; the image of Fullerton's arrow-pierced eye was intruding into his mind again, mixed up with the chest-constricting memory of the fire. Was this another crime to add to Landry's actions?

Stephanie moved to sit beside Margaret and took her hand.

Dering looked from Louisa to Burrell and said incredulously: 'You believe that Michael Landry killed Elaine and then John Fullerton because he discovered they were having an affair?'

'It's the working theory. Although we've found no incriminating evidence on either Elaine's or Fullerton's bodies, no helpful fingerprints on the arrows for example. We followed up a report by one of the archers that they saw a red car round about the time of the fire. Landry owned a red car and it's currently missing. There was no sign of forced entry at his house, no sign of a burglary, but when we searched the house we found Elaine's passport but not Michael's, which is suggestive. There's one further bit of evidence that may be helpful in time. A bow was handed in to us earlier today and I had a call about half an hour ago from Mr. St. John to say that a Welsh bowmaker had noticed when he got home that one of his stock was missing. They were all in his unlocked van or on display from Friday night onwards. It's possible that Landry could have taken the bow and the arrows on Saturday morning and tried to disguise Fullerton's bullet wound. The arrows were left in the body but he returned the bow to the campsite, hoping it would be overlooked. If so, then he may well have been creeping around the campsite over the weekend.'

'That's an unpleasant thought,' Shaw commented. 'He could have done anything.'

'Indeed. Such as buy two cans of petrol

at a garage nearby.'

'What? Have you found proof of that?' Dering asked in surprise.

'Slightly blurred CCTV footage that a neighbour has identified as being Landry.'

'So he really did start the fire.' Margaret spoke quietly but clearly and with intensity.

'I'm afraid that it looks that way. With the garage footage and your friend Miss Mudie's identification, there's growing evidence to support the theory. We have not in fact released that last piece of information, as I don't want to endanger her further.'

'Have you got a policeman in her room?' Margaret asked fiercely. 'She's just as much at risk as we are.'

Louisa answered her. 'Yes, we have. I really don't think Landry would risk it, but we have a uniformed officer there. She's quite safe.'

'But you don't think *we* are, or you wouldn't be here now with the cavalry on the way,' Dering stated bluntly.

Burrell didn't answer immediately. He got up and walked to the window. 'I don't like the fact that we don't know where Landry is and what state of mind he's in. The murder of Mrs. Landry could have been a moment's madness, although the use of a gun may point to premeditation if he had to buy one.'

Margaret was shaking her head. 'He likes guns, mostly shotguns for wild birds. He had a small collection when he was running Kempshott.'

Burrell thanked her for the information and continued. 'Even if he killed his wife on the spur of the moment, I think he must have arranged to meet Fullerton on that track on Saturday morning, fully prepared for murder. Then there's the attack on your cottage.'

'The attack on *us*, Inspector. He could have burnt the cottage down while we were out if he'd been lurking around. He wanted to kill us.'

Burrell looked bleak. 'You're right of course. Everything is pointing to a wish for revenge, and the fact that you have also been targeted makes me very concerned that Landry could be trying to settle all of his old scores. I understand that you and he fell out a few years ago, quite badly.'

Margaret looked round at the comfy old-fashioned room as if drawing solace from its familiar feel. 'When I sold my home, the home that had housed many generations of my family, I thought Michael Landry was going to take care of it. He was full of promises and flattery. It took a while for me to see him clearly but when I did, I knew he was a crook. I never found out all that he was up to but I suspected many things, including money laundering. He was never much of a success and he was starting to lose a lot of money. He began selling off the land, sacking the staff; anything to stop the rot. I hated it, absolutely hated it. He had no respect for Kempshott or for his employees. Many of the staff would come to see Janice and me and tell me how badly he was treating them. I took the trouble to get to know them, you see, unlike Michael. I knew I had to do something to get him and his awful wife out. I'm sorry, I know she's dead and I'm sure she didn't deserve that, but she was truly horrible toward the end.' She was looking down at her thin, veiny hands now and her voice was low.

'I had a flaming row with them both: me wanting them to sell up; them refusing point blank and telling me to keep my nose out of their business. Except they said it rather more rudely than that. The only card I had left to play was a guess, but it turned out to be a good one. I said that they left me with no option but to contact the police to report them for fraud, employing illegal immigrants and laundering money. I watched Michael's face carefully and he kept on sneering until I mentioned the last one. Then I saw him falter and I knew that I had him. I left before he could say any more but the next day he came down to the cottage, all smarm and false contrition. He said that they had decided it would be best to sell Kempshott and hoped we could be friends. I felt sickened by him, but I wanted him out.' She looked up at Burrell apologetically. 'I realise that I should have told the police of my suspicions but I couldn't face the prospect of a long investigation where I would have to go on seeing the Landrys. As soon as they agreed to go I set about luring Brendan here, and he's been just what I always wanted.' Her voice broke and Shaw saw there were tears in her eyes. 'I never dreamed that all this would happen.'

Burrell leaned over and gently took her hand in his. 'No one could have guessed that Landry would do these things. Most low-level criminals stay at that level. I believe that he was pushed over the edge by discovering the infidelity of his wife and his friend. Once he had passed that point and realised that with two murders to account for he would be spending most of his life behind bars, it looks like he didn't care much.' He sat back and said in a more practical tone of voice, 'What matters now is that we find him, quickly. What I need from you three —' He looked at Dering, Margaret and Stephanie. ' — is information about Kempshott and its grounds. It is possible that Landry's still hanging around here somewhere. Do you have any maps we can use?'

Margaret looked over at Dering. 'Brendan, my dear, I'm so glad we left the plan chest here rather than moving it to the cottage. I don't suppose you've had the chance to look through the contents, but it contains all the old maps that were made of the estate over the years.' She turned to address Burrell, her dark eyes bright and sharp. 'If that weasel is sneaking about out there we'll find him. It's time to fight back.'

8

The afternoon faded into evening, bringing shadows that crept over the lawns, slid round the trees and lingered at the edge of every oasis of light. Two policemen were patrolling the perimeter of the hotel and their presence seemed to heighten the sense of danger rather than provide comfort.

After Burrell's speech, the few remaining guests had elected to cut short their stay and within an hour they had been escorted off the premises. Shaw didn't blame them. Who would want to remain here knowing there was a murderer on the prowl? He knew that if he had not felt so involved, he would have high-tailed it too. It still puzzled him that the police were taking it so very seriously though. When they had held what Margaret called their council of war he had counted five officers, including two sniffer dogs with their handlers. He had managed to corner

161

Louisa for a few minutes and had asked her if this was a normal response. She had looked worried and was obviously debating whether or not to tell him.

'Come on, you can trust me not to spill the beans.'

'Okay, but you must keep this to yourself.' She fixed him with her grey eyes. 'When we searched Landry's house we found evidence of drug use. Not just cannabis either — this was a large amount of cocaine.'

'So you're worried Landry's out of his skull?'

'Yes, but it's not just that. We also found Fullerton's car a few hours ago. It had been left in the car park of the Basingstoke General Hospital.' Seeing Shaw was about to exclaim, she held up one finger in admonition. 'Just listen. Landry was seen on CCTV getting out of that car and hanging around the hospital. We think the police presence deterred him from trying anything there, but Kempshott is a softer target. As to the number of police the DI has brought in, there was an incident last year with a gunman — you must remember it, Nick? He shot three people before killing himself. The local force was criticised then for being slow to act, so this time they're not taking any chances.'

'Christ almighty! It hardly seems possible, any of this.' Shaw glanced around and saw that no one was watching them. He gathered Louisa into his arms, feeling the hard bulletproof vest digging into him. 'Please be careful,' he urged.

Her arms came up around him and held him just as tightly. 'I've been trained for this kind of thing, but yes, I will be very careful.' She broke the hold. 'It's probably all for nothing. If he has any sense he'll be miles away from here.'

'I hope to God he is!' Shaw replied fervently. 'The thought of him hiding out there in the dark, trying to finish Margaret off, makes my flesh crawl.'

Louisa nodded in agreement. 'It's not just her. It's quite possible he could harbour the same feelings about Dering. After all, he's making a real success of this place. From all that we've been able to find out, Landry has lurched from one dodgy scheme to the next all his life.' She looked back at the gathering of officers in the dining room where the briefing had been held. They were checking their radios and picking up the maps that Stephanie had photocopied for them. 'I have to get on, Nick. I'm sorry, it's going to be a long evening, night too possibly, but we have to use this chance of getting Landry while he's not thinking straight. Some of the things he's done have been pretty stupid, like trying to make the gunshot wound look like an arrow puncture. Cocaine can make people arrogant and convince them their ideas are brilliant. That's when we could get him.'

Shaw could see that although Louisa was tense, she was also excited about the prospect of a resolution to this case, while he was trying, rather unsuccessfully, to force down his fears. He made himself smile. 'I think the staff are going to start a poker game, so we'll have something to do.'

That had been something that had surprised and heartened him. While the guests had been in a hurry to leave, more of the hotel's staff had arrived. Evidently word had gone round and although the female employees had mostly had to go home to their families, the waiters, chef, gardener and some of the occasional staff had turned up in force. Many of them were foreign workers and it was obvious from their behaviour that they regarded their work colleagues as a stand-in family. The attack on Margaret and Janice had stirred up strong feelings and they wanted to show their support. Burrell had accepted that they weren't going to leave and had agreed they could stay as long as they didn't get in the way or try to be heroes. Nico, the chef, had set a couple of waiters to making sandwiches for everyone while he set up the tables in the bar for poker. 'It's like when we started here last year, before the opening,' he had said to Shaw, who was helping him shift the furniture. 'We did training in the day and hung out in the evenings.'

'Didn't Mr. Dering mind?' Shaw had asked.

'He liked it! Said it was cheaper team-building than running round a wood with paint guns. He joked it was a shame we had to open up to guests in the end. Margaret and Janice came up to join us a few times a week. Janice likes to play rummy but Margaret's a poker fiend.'

'That doesn't surprise me actually.' Shaw grinned.

'Well, it surprised us! She just watched at first, asking the occasional question about bidding. When she finally asked to join in we took it easy on her and she wiped the floor with us. After that she was one of the guys.' He laughed at the memory. 'I might have a chance tonight, if she doesn't play.'

Margaret had in fact elected to stay in Dering's office with Stephanie, an arrangement which Shaw suspected was a relief to Burrell. He remembered the brief exchange between them.

'I can have an officer drive you to the police station. You'll be perfectly safe there.'

'I won't be perfectly safe anywhere until that weasel is behind bars,' Margaret had protested vigorously. 'He could be hiding along the driveway with a sniper rifle for all you know! I'm far better off right here.'

'Okay, Mrs. Norden. I take your point.' Burrell had held up his hands in defeat. 'But I would ask that you stay here. This room appears to be one of the safest in the building. I'll keep one of my officers here with you.'

That had been a few hours ago. Now Shaw couldn't decide what to do with himself. Louisa had set off with the other officers and the dogs; Burrell was based in the dining room, co-ordinating the search; and Dering was wandering around the ground floor, unable to settle. Shaw had sat in the bar for a while, where an intense game of poker was in progress, although there were at least four men who were keeping a watchful eye on the windows and the entrance hall at all times, he noticed. All it was missing was a police helicopter whirling overhead with a strong searchlight. Standing up, he saw Dering staring out of the entrance hall window, and walked over to join him.

'How's Margaret?' Shaw asked.

Dering paused, considering his answer, then replied: 'Belligerent, gung-ho and angry. At least on the surface.' He turned from the window and sat down on one of the reception chairs. 'Underneath the bravado, I think she's horrified at the danger she feels she's brought to all of us.'

Shaw leaned against the desk. 'I guess that's understandable, despite it not being her fault. She seems to care a lot about the people here.'

'Oh she does. She's been involved with everything we've done here, including getting to know the staff. She did the hiring and firing when she ran Kempshott and knows a lot about people. That's one of the things that really hurt her about Michael Landry — he was able to deceive her, at least for a while. It knocked her confidence in herself quite badly.'

There was a burst of chatter from the bar as one hand finished and some players gave up their places to others.

'All this kind of thing has helped her a lot, you know.' Dering waved his hand towards the bar. 'She got to know us all and you could see she was happy that her home was run by lively and good-natured people. I'll never forget what she said to me when she first brought me here. 'I don't want Kempshott to be a museum. National Trust places are all right but there's no life in them. These big houses were meant to have lots of people — all sorts of people — living in them. They were meant to evolve.' I'm sure she would have liked to have children but her husband, who was also her second cousin, died young and she never remarried. I think her staff became her family instead. Michael and Elaine Landry wrecked that for her.' He sounded bitter for the first time since Shaw had met him. 'You know, most people are fine, decent folk but others are just complete bastards.'

'I don't need to ask which category the Landrys fall into, or fell I suppose in Elaine's case.' Shaw was fiddling with a paperknife.

'My God, she could be venomous! When it was clear that Margaret was going to get them out one way or another she contacted social services and tried to make out Margaret was losing her marbles. Luckily the GP told them it was a load of rubbish. Admittedly there are times now when she's not as sharp as she was, and when there's not a lot going on I've noticed that she can get tetchy and sometimes confused. I mean she is eighty-five. But I think it's partly boredom.'

'Well, she should be fine for the moment!' Shaw said.

In the dining room behind them they heard an excited exclamation from Burrell. 'Finally!'

Dering and Shaw hurried into the room. Burrell beckoned them in. His eyes were bright and he was obviously keyed up. 'The dogs picked up a scent in field three and they've found evidence that Landry has been there at some point in the last few days. He probably camped out there overnight and maybe at several points during the weekend.'

Shaw leaned over to look at the area Burrell was indicating on the map. It would have been easy for Landry to have walked over to the archery campsite and taken the bow and arrows. Presumably he had dumped the bow sometime late on Sunday night.

Burrell was speaking into the radio. 'Bring it up to the house. I want to see this.'

'What have they found?' Dering asked, his voice hovering between excitement and fear.

'A mobile phone.'

'Oh . . . what might that . . . I mean, do you think it's connected?' Dering said, expressing the same confusion that Shaw was feeling.

'Apparently the dogs were all over it so it must have Landry's scent on it. They're off trying to find where he went after that.' Burrell's radio crackled into life again and they heard Louisa's voice.

'This is definitely Fullerton's phone. There are a lot of text messages from Elaine Landry. It's pretty clear that she was going to leave her husband.'

'Well that's good corroborating evidence as to motive.'

'Hang on, sir. This one's different.' There was a pause and Shaw could imagine Louisa clicking through the messages. 'You'll have to see these but I think there's more to it, if you read between the lines.' They could hear that she was jogging now and it should only take a few minutes to reach the hotel.

'There's something here about 'fixing Michael'. We can go through it when I get there.'

Burrell had opened his mouth to speak but stopped as they all heard a shot and a scream from the other end of the hotel. The three men froze for an instant, then ran towards the office where Margaret was. Shaw got there first and found Stephanie holding the old lady and sobbing. Fearing the worst, he rushed to them and was relieved to see that Margaret was just comforting Stephanie. The police officer who had been with them was dragging one of the heavy bookcases, trying to pull it in front of the window that Shaw could see had been shattered.

'Help me get this window covered!' the officer commanded and together they blocked it, tipping half of the books out in the process.

Burrell and Dering came in a second later, the Detective Inspector still clutching his radio. 'What happened here? Is anybody hurt?' he asked.

'A shot came through the window, sir. Nearly hit Mrs. Norden. Here,' he said, indicating a hole in the other wall, 'you can see the bullet hole.'

'My God, he's really out there.' Shaw felt the full realisation of the situation hit him as strongly as a punch to the stomach. Burrell was talking rapidly into his radio, recalling his officers. The corridor had become crowded with the hotel staff, brought by the gunshot. Burrell looked at them in exasperation and told them all to *get* in here and *stay* in here. His normally smooth persona was fraying under the strain and Shaw guessed he had not truly expected Landry to risk anything with such a visible police presence. They all pressed into the smallish room, the earlier bravado now tinged with fear. Shaw found himself shuffled into a corner by the door, and he could hear Burrell outside in the corridor communicating with the other officers. He was checking in with all of them in turn. When it came to Sergeant West there was a delay; then her voice came quietly over the radio.

'I can see Landry, sir.'

'Do not engage, do you hear me? The

suspect is armed and dangerous. I repeat, do not engage. Fall back to the hotel if it's safe to do so. I'm calling for armed response.' Burrell spoke urgently.

'I'm not sure if I can get there. He's between me and the hotel but I don't think he's seen me. I'm on the path to the campsite.' She sounded controlled but Shaw felt panic welling up inside him. He pressed his ear close to the door to hear better.

'Then stay where you are. If you can still see him, watch him, but do not follow. Everyone here is safe; he can't reach them.'

'Yes, sir. I'll keep you updated.'

Burrell started to make a call to the station to call for armed backup.

Shaw didn't know what to do. None of the others in the office had heard the exchange and were either waiting pensively or talking about the shot through the window. He knew that Louisa would want him to stay put, but he felt such a nervous energy running through him. He desperately wanted to see what was going on; to help her.

His agonising was short-lived. There

was another gunshot that made everyone jump. It sounded a little way off and certainly hadn't been directed towards the blocked office window. Shaw heard running feet outside the door and then his body took over. Without thinking, he darted out of the door and quietly followed Burrell, who was running to the dining room to look out.

'Report in, all of you. Did anyone see what just happened?' he demanded. From the replies that Shaw could make out, none of them had. There was no reply from Louisa. 'Sergeant West, please respond.' Still nothing. Then a different voice came out of the radio.

'I want you to call your men off, and the dogs too.'

'Who is this?' Burrell barked harshly.

'I have the policewoman with me. She's bleeding and will need help, so you *will* do as I say or she might just bleed to death while you argue.'

Shaw froze at the words, his heart plummeting. There was only one woman on the team. He didn't know whether to rush forward and demand that Burrell do something to save her, or to hang back and let the DI do his job. His shocked paralysis kept him in place to hear Burrell's reply.

'Mr. Landry? What is it you want?'

'Well, I could ask for a king's ransom and a helicopter, but I don't want to hang around here much longer.' The voice was smooth and contemptuous. 'I'll settle for safe passage away from the grounds. Shortly we will be leaving in my car and I want all of your men to stay back at the hotel. If I get stopped anywhere the woman dies. If I see anyone following me, she dies. If I get away from here without any interference then, at some point, I will release her.'

'I need proof that my sergeant is alive,' Burrell said. He sounded steady but he was pacing up and down by the window.

There was a pause and then Louisa was speaking, her voice tremulous. 'I'm here, sir.'

Then Landry was back. 'You have your proof. I want my guarantee.'

Shaw didn't stop to hear anything more. The paralysis had gone, replaced by rage and fear. He backed carefully away down the side passage that led to the kitchen. There was no way he was going to let Landry drive off with Louisa. The likelihood of her either bleeding to death or being killed was too high. For days he had felt that events were moving out of his control; felt out of his depth. Yes, he could be useful, but only on the sidelines. Now, though, the uncertainty seemed to have been burned out of him by his anger.

He ran to the door that led out of the kitchen. It was locked of course, but he remembered Nico had chosen to slide the large bolt across rather than find the key. He quickly pulled it back and opened the door, stepping out into the dark court-yard beyond. There were no lights out there tonight. No one had been around to put them on, but that suited him. There was no one in sight and the way to the car park looked clear. Shaw's mind was working overtime, running through the possibilities. Louisa had been coming up the path when she saw Landry, who had presumably been going away from the hotel after shooting at Margaret. There was no way he would have left his car in the car park, so it must be hidden somewhere else.

Shaw reached his car and quietly opened the boot. He pulled out his bow and quiver and strung the bow. His plan was to enter the wooded area that started by the car park and follow it down towards the campsite, hoping to spot Landry somewhere along the way.

It was only a guess that they had gone in this direction but it proved to be a good one. He slipped between the trees, carefully making his way downhill, and by the time his eyes were accustomed to the dark he began to hear sounds. Someone else was out there, stumbling from time to time and breaking twigs underfoot.

Shaw strained his eyes and caught a glimpse of moving figures. Landry was making use of the tree cover too. Squinting, he could see a smaller figure being towed along. Thank God, she was alive! He had to stop himself shouting with relief. His heart raced, more with stress than exertion, and he took deep breaths to try and calm it. The fear that he could endanger Louisa rather than save her was uppermost in his thoughts and he knew there was no room for error.

The trees grew thickly here and the scrubby plants underfoot made it hard to keep up his pace. He could hear Landry scrambling through the wood a little way ahead and he caught an occasional flash of Louisa's fair hair. If she had been trying to talk to Landry at first, following the guidelines for engaging a captor, she must have given it up. From what little Shaw could make out, her right arm was either strapped to her body, or perhaps tucked into her jacket. Presumably that was where the bullet had hit her. The sound of the shot was still echoing round in his head, coupled with an image his mind had generated of the awful moment. Even though it stabbed at his heart, he welcomed it. It wound the anger tightly inside him and gave him the adrenaline to keep going.

The clouds had drawn back, allowing moonlight to filter through the canopy of leaves overhead, and he was glad he had decided not to take a torch. His eyes had adjusted to the low light, and with his dark clothes and hair he was almost invisible. The beam of Landry's torch bobbed and wavered, making it easy to follow them, but he could only guess at where they were going.

Landry seemed to be slowing a little and Shaw had to switch to a walk to keep a good distance between them. The bow had been awkward at first and he had wondered whether he should just drop it, but he felt loath to give up his only weapon. He was getting used to manoeuvring with it now and took some comfort from the familiar feel of it in his hand. In Shaw's mind the possibility that Landry might still kill Louisa kept rising to the surface. He tried to convince himself that Landry needed her to get away, to get to the coast or something, but that depended on the man acting logically. Remembering Landry's actions to date, he could not convince himself that logic was still there. The only thing he could do was to follow them and hope for a chance to rescue Louisa.

9

'Keep walking!' Landry's voice sounded shockingly close.

Shaw saw that Louisa was flagging. She stumbled and nearly fell but Landry pulled her upright. If she did fall over, Shaw realised it might give him the chance to challenge Landry, though he still didn't know how to do it. If he shot an arrow, what would be the consequences? If it killed him it would save Louis but he could easily miss — could even hit Louisa. Maybe he could get close enough to jump Landry and knock the gun out of his hand? But again, if Landry spotted him he might follow through with his threat to kill Louisa. Shaw was working hard to keep the panic down; it was threatening to overwhelm him.

'How far is it?' Louisa sounded faint and strained and her voice tore at Shaw.

'You're not that badly hurt. Keep moving,' Landry ordered impatiently.

'Anyway, we're close now. You won't have the pleasure of my company for much longer.' The oily tone of his voice set Shaw's teeth on edge.

If Landry got Louisa in the car, Shaw wouldn't be able to do much to stop him. He began to psych himself up to launch an attack before they got that far, but then paused. Would Landry be able to drive while holding a gun on Louisa? Even if he planned to, he would surely be likely to be at his most vulnerable while getting into the car. He felt his spirits lift a little. If he could take advantage of that brief time, there was still a chance.

He continued to follow at a distance and now he could detect a familiar smell — charred wood and water. They must be nearing the burnt-out cottage. That meant that Landry's car was probably parked somewhere along the track at the back. He would have to take a risk if he was going to help her, and he knew he could be faster than them.

Slipping further back into the trees, he skirted around the cottage in the opposite direction to Landry, ducking under the yellow-and-black police tape to get through. To his relief he saw a car. Landry had driven it almost into the ditch by a shed at the back of the garden. It wouldn't be seen easily from most angles, but was still a risky thing to have done with the police searching. Maybe his realisation that they were after him had tipped him into taking even greater risks. Either that or he really was high on cocaine. The shot at Margaret earlier had been stupid and had achieved nothing. Grabbing Louisa did at least have an element of logic. He could conceivably use her to get away, although surely the authorities would be looking out for him at all points where he could leave the country. Whatever Landry's current state of mind, Shaw was not going to have long to decide how to act.

The beam of the torch was coming closer and Shaw looked around hurriedly for a hiding place. The moonlight was shining strongly on the track and he only had seconds before Landry would be able to see him. He crouched down beside the boot of the car, still clutching his bow.

He was only just in time.

Louisa came into view first, her head down and clutching her right arm to her chest. Shaw pressed himself back to the far end of the car and saw Landry bundle her into the back seat. The torch was switched off and dropped somewhere in the car. Landry slammed the door and turned to the driver's door.

Shaw knew it was now or never. He surged up from the ground and leaped forward, bringing the bow over Landry's head and pulling back hard. Landry let out a gurgling shout of shock and pain, his hands flying up to tug the wooden stave away from his throat. He hadn't dropped the gun but for the moment he seemed to be focused on escaping from the strangling hold Shaw had on him.

Knowing he had to get the gun out of the way, Shaw changed tack. Releasing his hold on the bow, he abruptly pushed Landry forward onto the bonnet of the car, managing to sweep his feet out from under him. Landry's chin hit the metal heavily and Shaw was able to grab the gun. He had never had any interest in firearms and he remembered a line from some film or other — 'A weapon you don't know how to use is a gift to your enemy.' Deciding that he agreed, he drew his arm back and threw the gun as far as he could into the neighbouring field.

Landry was coughing and gasping for air, his hands at his bruised neck. Shaw heaved him round and pushed him down until he was sitting on the ground, his back against one of the front tyres. Seeing the man clearly for the first time in the moonlight, he was shocked to recognise him — not from the polished publicity photograph Stephanie had shown him, but from Saturday morning. This was the man he had seen looking over the lists of archers when Louisa had turned up. He remembered the scruffy grey beard and shooting jacket that had seen better days.

'So you've caught me. Well done,' Landry rasped sarcastically. 'Citizen's arrest and all that, as I can tell you're not police.' His dark eyes were mocking and arrogant with not a hint of remorse or fear.

Shaw could well understand the lack of

remorse, but the fact that Landry didn't seem in the least worried was perversely worrying *him*. Surely the man should at least be a bit concerned that he had been apprehended. He was unsure what to do next. He supposed he should tie Landry up somehow and get the police down there. Then, with a swell of guilt, he thought of Louisa. For a moment, the shock of capturing Landry had pushed her from his mind.

'Louisa!' he called. 'Are you all right?'

There came a muffled curse from the interior of the car, then her voice. 'Nick, what's happening?'

'I've got Landry,' he replied.

'Jesus, Nick, well done! We need to call the others. Where's your phone?' She still hadn't sat up and her voice was strained.

Shaw felt for his pocket but realised that he didn't have his jacket on. 'I don't have it. Can't we use your radio?' There was no answer. 'Louisa!' he called, seriously worried.

Landry started to laugh. He hadn't moved since Shaw had forced him to the ground, but now he shifted his legs to a seemingly more comfortable position. 'Her radio is somewhere in the woods back there.'

'What?' Shaw looked at his captive with anger.

'I chucked it. If they set the dogs on us, that will hold their attention for a bit.' Landry raised an eyebrow sarcastically. 'You have a bit of a dilemma I'd say. Do you help the lady or keep an eye on me?'

Shaw was looking around him for inspiration and saw the fallen bow. He wouldn't be able to pick it up, nock an arrow and bring it to bear on Landry before the man could be up and away, but there was another way to use it. He had to be quick. Before Landry could react, Shaw pulled him forwards, pushing his face onto the track. Then he hauled him towards the rear of the car and opened the back door. Landry was struggling but was off balance and couldn't get enough purchase to throw Shaw off. The interior light showed Louisa was lying on the back seat on her good arm and breathing slowly. Desperately, Shaw shoved Landry along the floor on his front, wedging him in the footwell. Placing his foot on Landry's back, he heaved at the bow to unstring it and then bound Landry's wrists tightly with the waxy string. Landry cursed and writhed.

'Louisa, wake up!' Shaw stroked her face and she responded weakly. There was a large, sticky stain of blood on her clothes and her arm was dripping. 'We don't have a radio or a phone, love. I'm going to have to get you out of here. Where did he shoot you?' It was a needless question for the answer was obvious, but he wanted to get her talking.

She opened her eyes and took in a long breath. 'Sorry, I must have blanked out.' She was trying to sound normal but the pain and shock were evident. 'The bullet's in my upper arm. It didn't hit an artery but I've lost quite a lot of blood.'

'I'll drive you back up to the hotel. The other officers must know first aid and we can get help from there.' Shaw was relieved to see the car keys were still in the ignition.

'Okay, let's go then. Get me in the front. I don't want to be here with him.'

Louisa stared down at Landry with a look of disgust.

'You sound like my wife,' Landry said, his voice slightly muffled. 'I shot her too.'

'Shut up!' Shaw barked at him.

'He's trying to create an opportunity. Just ignore him,' Louisa advised.

Shaw helped her into the passenger seat. Starting up the car, he headed along the track. He could feel the adrenaline still pumping round his body. He didn't feel like they were out of the woods yet but if he got them back to the hotel, Louisa could get to hospital and have a transfusion, Landry would be arrested, and there was absolutely no way he would avoid a very long prison sentence. Margaret and the others would be safe.

The road was bumpy and he didn't want to go too fast given Louisa's state. It curved round to the left, heading back up to the main road.

Landry continued to talk for a while, trying to provoke a response, but Shaw managed not to rise to his provocations. Just a bit further and they would be home and dry.

'Stop the car!' Louisa suddenly gasped.

'What is it?' Shaw asked, his heart hammering.

'Nick, they might shoot you. Stop the car!'

He did so and turned to her anxiously. 'What do you mean?'

'I know Burrell will have called the armed response unit when Margaret was shot at. If they see you driving Landry's car, with me slumped in the front seat, they'll assume you're him. We have to get out.'

In the back, Landry laughed. 'Finally worked it out, did you? I was rather hoping you wouldn't. 'Police shoot have-a-go hero' would have made a good headline. Almost as good as 'Mass murderer escapes, police baffled', which sadly seems to be less likely than I would have wanted.'

Shaw felt his hands tightening on the steering wheel. The urge to smash Landry's face in was becoming hard to resist. 'Okay, we need to walk the rest of the way. I can carry you if necessary, but what shall we do with him?'

They exchanged worried looks. It

would be impossible to herd their prisoner with Louisa injured as she was. Shaw briefly regretted throwing the gun away. The puzzle of the farmer who has to find a way to transport a fox, a chicken and a bag of grain across the river came to him. In their case, if he frog-marched Landry to the police, Louisa's condition could worsen in his absence. If he took her, Landry could escape. He couldn't leave them together and go to get help; Louisa was too weakened and would be at risk.

'Is the boot of the car an enclosed one?' Louisa asked.

Shaw craned round to look. 'I think so. You want me to put him in there?'

'It's the only thing I can think of,' she said, her voice faint.

'Right.' Shaw got out. He wasn't sure how easy that would be. Landry was in no mood to co-operate and had started complaining vociferously at the thought of being locked in the boot of the car. Shaw opened the boot in preparation, then the rear door swung open and he narrowly missed being kicked in the stomach. Landry had somehow managed to turn over onto his back and had lashed out with his feet, although his hands were still tied. Shaw offered a silent prayer of thanks to Smithy, who had made that string for him last year and made it well. He made a grab for Landry's feet and caught them at the ankles. Giving a heave, he pulled Landry hard so that he half slid, half fell out of the car.

'Hey! Watch what you're doing! I'll have you for GBH!' Landry yelled.

'Shut up, you bastard! I could have put an arrow in you earlier and I'm beginning to wish I had.' Shaw dragged him round to the boot he had already opened and roughly pushed him inside. He could see it was a tight fit, but Landry's well-being was not his priority at the moment. Ignoring his protestations, he firmly shut the boot.

★   ★   ★

It took a very long twenty minutes for Shaw to carry Louisa to the edge of the hotel gardens with the moon lighting their way. She had tried to walk a bit but it became increasingly clear that she was near collapse. He had tried to keep her talking at first, but he soon ran out of breath himself and concentrated on getting to help as soon as he could. Her head was curled into his shoulder and he could smell the blood that had begun to seep into his own clothes. Before they left the car he had done his best to bandage her arm, but the constant jolting of their progress wasn't helping.

Upon reaching the edge of the lawn, he began to shout for help. There were no police visible at first but the moment he called out they rushed towards him. He saw that at least one had a gun before his legs gave way and he stumbled, almost dropping Louisa. They quickly took her out of his arms and there was a tense moment when he wondered if they thought he was Landry. Then Burrell was there, his usually smooth features oscillating between relief and rage.

'You bloody idiot! You could have got both of you killed!' he shouted. 'And what's happened to Landry?'

'He's in the boot of his car, on the farmer's track. Unless he's Harry Houdini he's still there.'

'Go and get him!' Burrell told two of the officers who had joined them. 'I take it he doesn't have a gun anymore?' he asked Shaw impatiently.

'It's in a field somewhere. I don't think he would be able to find it, even if he got out.'

'All right. Get inside; we can get you looked over.'

The officer who had taken Louisa had brought her into the hotel and when Shaw staggered in, she was on a sofa in the lounge. Her eyes were shut and she was paler than he had ever known her. He hovered there, not knowing what to do, until another officer — Gibson, he thought — took his arm and steered him to a seat.

'Stay here for the moment. The ambulance should be here soon and you can go with her to the hospital.'

Shaw nodded wearily. He slumped down into the soft armchair. The adrenaline that had kept him going had

194

drained away, leaving him exhausted. He wondered vaguely where Dering was. It surprised him to realise that it had been less than an hour since he had slipped out of the hotel to rescue Louisa. He would have to go back in the morning and find his bow. He had left it near the cottage when he'd used the string to tie Landry's hands together. He'd have to tell Smithy, St. John and all the others about what had happened, and there was sure to be another interview with the police, but for the present his only concern was Louisa. As long as she was okay he could cope with all the rest.

He had been sitting there watching her for a couple of minutes when he heard a commotion outside. Looking out of the window, he saw that two policemen were escorting a very dishevelled Landry along the drive. Shaw sighed with relief. He had begun to worry that he may have somehow escaped. Burrell had gone out to see Landry and Shaw heaved himself out of the chair to watch. Although Landry looked like he had been dragged through a hedge, he was still collected and sauntered next to the policemen as if he was taking a stroll.

There was a sound of feet and voices from behind him, and Shaw turned to see all the hotel staff who had been kept in the office pouring into the entrance hall to see Landry's capture. Dering came out, wheeling Margaret in the office chair. After he checked that Louisa was being looked after, Shaw joined them in the hall.

Margaret was looking daggers at Landry, who raised a hand in a mocking greeting.

'He doesn't give a damn, does he?' she said. 'Look at him, smirking at us.'

'Where's a little police brutality when you need it,' Dering agreed.

'That's him out of it at least. Away from here,' Shaw said.

'I just wish he didn't look so damned pleased with himself. Like it's all a big joke. You wouldn't think he was a murderer who had just lost everything, would you?' Margaret glared angrily out of the window.

The officers had put Landry in the car. Shaw noticed that he had been hand-cuffed and wondered briefly what they had done with his bowstring.

Burrell was talking with them and looking back occasionally at the hotel. Then he opened the door and walked in. 'Mr. Dering, could I have a word please? And with you too, Mr. Shaw?' he asked. He looked strangely worried and spoke first to Shaw. 'How was Landry when you caught him? I mean, emotionally?'

'Arrogant, unrepentant, unpleasant,' Shaw answered without hesitation.

'Not particularly annoyed that he had been caught, then?'

'I thought he was angry but didn't want to show it. I'm sure he would have run away if he'd had the chance, but no, he didn't seem as upset as I would have thought.'

'Why are you asking?' Dering put in curiously.

'I've seen a lot of criminals when they've just been arrested and he's worrying me. Okay, he doesn't want to show weakness, but there's a . . . ' Burrell broke off, trying to find the right words. 'An air of triumph about him. Even now he just drawled about supposing he should call a lawyer and asking if we had comfortable beds at the station.'

'Do you think he might be intending to kill himself; deprive you of the satisfaction of a trial?' Shaw asked rather sceptically.

'It's a thought, but no. I suspect he has something else up his sleeve. There isn't any way he could have got into the hotel, is there — when he was around here earlier?'

'Christ! You don't think he's put a bomb here or something!' Dering exclaimed.

'I've no reason to believe that he did anything like that, but I would like to test something out. I want to bring Landry in here and see what happens. If he *has* done anything then he might betray signs of stress.'

Dering looked uncomfortable. 'I don't want him anywhere near Margaret.'

'Neither do I. By the looks of her he might not survive the encounter,' Burrell said with a twist of his lips. 'No, we'll keep her out of the way. What I suggest is that we move everyone outside and take Landry round to the kitchen door. He won't realise what we're doing until the last moment. The car can go round that way as if it's heading out. It's just a precaution, but I'll be happier once we've done it.'

Within the space of five minutes the swap had been accomplished. All the hotel staff were on the lawn and the car with Landry in it had pulled away. The ambulance had arrived and Shaw was just getting in with Louisa when they heard shouts. It seemed Landry had tried to make a half-hearted run for it but had been stopped by a German Shepherd released by one of the police-dog handlers.

The arrogant, controlled man from earlier was gone. This Landry was shouting and struggling. Had the inevitability of prison finally hit him? Had the cocaine worn off? Or had Burrell been right? Shaw suddenly remembered Landry's remark about 'Mass murderer escapes'.

'What's happening?' Louisa asked, frustrated that she couldn't see anything.

'Landry's lost it, I think.'

'I want to know more than that! Find out for me!'

The paramedic who was assessing Louisa

shook his head. 'No more excitement for you for a while. We need to get moving. You've lost a fair amount of blood and that bullet has definitely outstayed its welcome.' He pulled the doors shut and signalled to his colleague to drive off.

They pulled away and Shaw watched the lights of Kempshott recede out of the back window for a long time as they made their way down the drive. Then he turned his gaze and attention to Louisa. He laughed with relief at the frustrated expression on her face. Even the pain of being shot and the exhaustion of all she had gone through that night didn't stop her being a detective — or 'officially nosy person', as she often put it.

'What is it?' she asked, giving him a funny look.

'Nothing. I just love you.'

She sighed. 'I love you too, Nick, but you and I are going to have a talk about stupid heroics when I'm better.'

'Whatever you say.'

'And I want you to call Dering or someone and find out what happened back there.'

'No problem.' He grinned. The stress was falling away now he knew she was safe.

'And . . . '

'That's enough,' the paramedic broke in. 'You're not in danger but you still need to rest.'

The ambulance sped into the night, safe and reassuring. It was not far to the hospital but even so, Shaw was asleep by the time they got there.

10

To her great annoyance, Louisa had been told to stay in hospital for a couple of nights while she recovered from the operation to remove the bullet. Shaw, on the other hand, agreed wholeheartedly with the doctors. The morning after Landry's dramatic capture Burrell had come to see Louisa. Shaw had stayed overnight at the hospital, lying across three chairs in the canteen. Returning to Louisa's ward with a cup of coffee, he saw Burrell ahead of him in the corridor and sped up. He was just as eager to hear the latest news as Louisa.

'Good morning, to both of you,' Burrell said as Shaw jogged into the room. There was only one other patient in the ward that morning, in a bed in the far corner, so they had plenty of space to pull up chairs.

Louisa was looking much perkier now and the colour was returning to her cheeks. Her arm was, however, in a sling and she would have to let it rest and recover for weeks.

'So? What happened last night after we left?' she demanded impatiently.

Burrell crossed his legs and smoothed his pristine trousers, considering his words. 'Well, I don't know if you were aware of this, Sergeant West, but I had a suspicion that Landry's behaviour was all wrong when we picked him up — too smug, too self-assured. As he had been hiding on the grounds of Kempshott for several days I got worried that he may have done something to sabotage the house as his final act of revenge. The wild shot at Margaret Norden through the window seemed foolish, even for Landry, who has an inflated opinion of his own cleverness.

'Then I remembered. The little courtyard area outside that window is definitely functional rather than decorative. The air-conditioning units are located there, along with the main electrical junction box. Could Landry have been doing something else there when he decided to take a shot at Margaret? I thought it was worth a brief experiment and arranged for Landry to be brought round to the kitchen door and into the house.

'The moment he got wind of what we were doing he started to protest — thought up all sorts of reasons why he couldn't enter the house, from claiming Dering had a restraining order on him to wittering on about a ghost. When I confronted him about it he finally confessed, as long as he could get back into the car. On Sunday night he had tried to sabotage the electrics in order to start an electrical fire that would do a lot of damage before anyone discovered it. He knows hardly anything about wiring so all he managed to do was to interfere with the power supply.'

'Stephanie was complaining there was something up with it!' Shaw said. 'Just before everything kicked off yesterday.'

'There must be more to it than that though. He wouldn't have been scared to enter the hotel just for that,' Louisa insisted.

'You're right. Landry had cooked up another idea while he was sleeping rough. He had heard that phosphine gas was lethal and tried to introduce it into the air-conditioning system. That's what he had been doing yesterday evening. The air-con unit is in the courtyard too. While he was setting up his gas attack he saw Margaret in the office. Once he had done what he came to do he decided to take a shot at her on the off-chance of being lucky.'

'My God, so did he really poison the air?' Louisa exclaimed in alarm. 'Is everyone all right?'

'Don't worry, they're all fine, though if he had managed to do it right it could have been catastrophic when we had all of those people crowded into Dering's office. He botched the job. Very little of the gas actually entered the system, thankfully. That's his problem all over — he doesn't do things properly.'

'He still succeeded in killing two people,' Shaw reminded Burrell who he thought was looking too pleased with himself.

'True. He did,' Burrell admitted. 'He told us about that too, once we were back at the station. He'd suspected his wife, Elaine, of playing around for a couple of months. Nothing had gone right for him since he'd sold Kempshott and the remaining money was dwindling fast. Elaine was increasingly critical of him for a long time, blaming him for their situation, but then she changed — stopped complaining so much and was nicer. Knowing her as well as he did, Landry smelled a rat. The clincher came when he answered a call on her mobile when she was in the bath. It was about a life-insurance policy she had taken out on him without his knowledge. Going through her phone, he also found messages to John Fullerton and put two and two together.'

'So they were planning to kill him and claim the insurance?' Louisa said.

'Not only that. When Landry confronted her about it last week she said it was all Fullerton's idea and that he intended to do the same with his wife, although we only have Landry's word for it at the moment and I wouldn't take that on trust. So Landry got angry enough to kill Elaine and set up a meeting with Fullerton, sending texts from her mobile saying she wanted to see him. He'd been up to his eyes in cocaine all weekend and got more erratic as the days went on. He was pretty annoyed to find that the quiet, out-of-the way place he had chosen for his meeting had become a 'bloody festival' — his words not mine. He nearly changed his plans entirely, but he had come too far to countenance turning back and after a bit he thought the archery might actually be useful to him; might muddy the waters.'

'When did he decide to kill Margaret? Was it always planned?' Louisa asked.

'It was on Saturday that he hatched that plot. He killed Fullerton early on Saturday morning and kept the body in his car. He'd found out about the blind shoot when he was talking to one of the archers on Friday night and found the idea amusing. He dumped the body in the spinney and stuck it with arrows. He did try to use the stolen bow to shoot them in but found it too difficult. He stayed lurking around long enough to see that Fullerton had been discovered, then stayed away for the rest of that day.

'I think that his glee at having killed two enemies was now fuelling him. What if he could get even with all of them? That seems to have been his motivation now. The next obvious target was Margaret. He says she wrecked everything for him — his marriage, his livelihood. He bought the petrol and waited until she and Janice were out of the house. Then he broke in and took his time soaking the upper level of the cottage with petrol.'

Shaw butted in: 'Why just upstairs?'

'Landry reasoned that if the downstairs was similarly treated, the smell would be so strong that they wouldn't go into the house. He also wanted to get out of there alive himself. He incapacitated both women and then flicked a match up the stairs. Leaving them to burn to death.'

'There can't have been much of a gap between him leaving and us arriving. When did he know that he had failed?'

'Not until the story reached the news that evening and there was no mention of fatalities.'

Louisa let out a deep breath. 'My God, what a bastard!'

'There's no chance he'll get let off, is there?' Shaw said. 'He must be at least a little mad, don't you think?'

Burrell shook his head. 'This is moral aberration, not mental aberration, and he should get a long enough sentence that he'll be too old to be of any danger to the public. That's if he lives to be released.' He looked critically at Louisa. 'I think I should leave you to get some more rest. We'll need you — and you too, Nick — for the trial, but I don't know when that will be.' He rose to his feet and shook hands with Shaw. 'I'll send someone round for your statements, but that will be later on. If you haven't been put off by recent events, I would suggest you stay at Kemp-shott while Louisa recovers. It's perfectly free from any gas or other substances.' He started to leave but turned back to speak to Louisa. 'There'll be a commendation for you if I have anything to do with it. You did very well.' And with that, he left.

★   ★   ★

'My dear. Welcome back!' The joyful shout reached them as Shaw pulled up outside the hotel.

Shaw had collected Louisa from hospital and brought her to Kempshott for their final night before going home. He had stayed there in the intervening few days, visiting Louisa, relaxing with his new friends and trying to return to normal.

Margaret and Stephanie had set a table out on the lawn and settled Louisa into a comfortable chair that someone had obviously dragged out from the lounge for her. Louisa smiled as she sank into the soft cushions and looked appreciatively at the table. 'Hospital food certainly didn't include scones and — my God, is that really Simnel cake?'

'Eat up — you need to look after yourself for a while,' Margaret urged her.

For at least ten minutes they did just that; then Louisa sat back, cradling her tea cup. 'So, how have things been here?' she asked.

'Fine, now that weasel is out of the picture. You should have seen him when they dragged him off in the end. He was a blubbering wreck.'

She smiled with satisfaction. 'That's the image I'll retain of him, and deservedly so.'

'Good. You'll probably have to give evidence against him in due course and he'll be as smart as they come for that.'

'And I can just picture him as he was that time and it won't bother me at all,' Margaret said firmly.

'We have more cake if you want it, Nick,' Stephanie offered. He had been hoovering up the crumbs without noticing.

'Sorry, it's just so good. Who made this one?'

'Nico, but from my recipe,' Margaret answered. 'When we get Janice back then we can really get going. She's a brilliant baker. Brendan's going to take me up there tomorrow and I can tell her about our plans.' Margaret looked a little sad but determined. 'I've been down to see the cottage and I really can't imagine living there again, even with it all rebuilt. I've discussed it with Brendan and Stephanie and I'm going to use the insurance money to transform the old stables into a nice little place for us, with some of the area still kept for horses if Stephanie ever gets her way. We'll stay here in the hotel while it's being done and I'm helping out with a few things.'

'Margaret likes baking and she's teaching Nico some of the English classics,' Stephanie explained.

'Most of which are being eaten by Nick, it seems,' Margaret said, laughing.

'I'm so glad it's working out for you, after such awful events,' Louisa said.

'Well, you can't get to my age without some sad things happening, but if you have the right attitude you can overcome them. I actually feel more alive now than I did before. I think I was getting bored. You must keep the brain active or it just turns to jelly. Of course, having the right friends helps immeasurably too.' She smiled at Shaw and Louisa. 'And you are most definitely part of the family now. If you both hadn't been so brave, who knows what might have happened.' She considered for a moment and added slightly wistfully: 'Although, you know, I would have put an arrow in Michael Landry when I had the chance if it had been me.'

All three of her listeners chorused: 'We know!'

★ ★ ★

A lot later, Louisa and Shaw were once again sitting outside, but this time they were having a last drink before retiring to bed.

'How do you feel, really?' Shaw asked.

'Peaceful actually,' answered Louisa. 'I know there's work still to be done on the case, mostly a lot of writing up, but right now I feel very relaxed.'

Shaw thought that she finally looked it too. The keyed-up excitement that he had seen in her was gone, for the moment at least. No doubt it would return the next time she was working on something big, but for now she was back to being her off-duty self. 'It's been a very strange time, but we made some good friends here and I'd like to come back sometime,' he said.

'Me too. I've never been rescued before and I think that makes this place rather special.' Louisa sat gazing out at the fields and woods, then added: 'Although I don't want you to make a habit of it. I nearly had a heart attack when you appeared like an avenging angel.'

'You know that I couldn't have just

stayed out of it, not when he'd hurt you.' Shaw looked steadily at her. 'Yes, it was foolhardy, but I won't apologise for it.'

Louisa interlaced her fingers with his. 'I wouldn't want you to. I was in real trouble.' She smiled and tilted her head to one side. 'Perhaps we could do a job swop. You hunt down the villains, and I'll swan off to write about travel.'

'No chance! Reviewing is a dangerous job. One word out of place and you'll never write in this town again.'

'And you would falter in the face of all those hours spent eating doughnuts on stakeouts,' she teased him in return. 'Better stick to what we're good at.'

'Right. You detect crime, I detect poor laundry systems and service. Sounds like a workable division of labour to me.' He saw she had finished her drink and took both empty glasses. 'Time for bed, I think.'

'Agreed,' Louisa replied and they left the gently scented garden.

Dering was manning the front desk and taking a phone call. He raised a hand to bid them goodnight. Going past the lounge, they saw a mismatched couple playing cards.

Margaret was seated opposite Nico and was flipping her hand face up on the table.

'My straight beats your kings.'

Nico looked at her cards and shook his head in disbelief. 'You're a terrible woman, Margaret Norden.' He grinned at her. 'I wish I'd met you years ago.'

Shaw steered Louisa to the lift. 'No arguments — you're taking it easy at the moment. No tearing up and down stairs.' He had a last glimpse of the friendly scene in the lounge and felt a sudden stab of emotion. What if Landry had succeeded in his plans? All of this would have been obliterated. His hands had clenched involuntarily and Louisa noticed.

As usual she guessed his thoughts. 'If I've learned anything as a police officer,' she said 'it's that you *can* make a difference, sometimes all the difference in the world. One time I was struggling with a morass of conflicting evidence, trying to tell the liars apart from the merely deluded. I imagined myself as one of my arrows, flying straight to the target, piercing the truth at the centre of the lies. There will always be other crimes, other murders, but I just concentrate on one at a time, and when I've finished it I have a while when I properly enjoy the satisfaction of having made the world a little safer.' She took his hand in hers. 'Don't dwell on what might have been. You did some amazing things this past week and a dangerous man is out of circulation because of it.'

Shaw nodded slowly. 'Okay, I'll try not to think about the what-ifs.'

They had reached their room and Louisa flopped carefully on to the bed. 'Ah, I'm going to miss this bed when we leave.'

'Well, I gave the beds a particular mention.' Shaw handed her a couple of typewritten pages.

'You finished the review!'

'Stephanie let me use one of their computers to write it up, which probably contravenes the reviewers' code of honour, if there is one, but it was extremely useful.'

'Read it to me,' Louisa commanded. 'I want to lie here and do nothing.'

'All right.' Shaw cleared his throat and settled down in a chair.

'Kempshott House Hotel was originally built in the 1790s for the Perceval family and period features abound in the seventeen guest rooms. Falconry, archery and clay pigeon shooting can be enjoyed on arrangement with the front desk and it has all the amenities and charm you would expect from a country house hotel. What you might not expect is the passion with which this hotel is run . . . ' He lowered his voice and then stopped as he saw that Louisa had fallen asleep. He set down the pages and watched her breathing softly. With Louisa safely beside him and the hotel warm with laughter and goodwill, he knew that Landry's toxic hatred had been defeated. As Louisa had said, there would be other murders at other times, but right here and now he felt at peace.

THE END

We do hope that you have enjoyed reading this large print book.

Did you know that all of our titles are available for purchase?

We publish a wide range of high quality large print books including:
Romances, Mysteries, Classics
General Fiction
Non Fiction and Westerns

Special interest titles available in large print are:
The Little Oxford Dictionary
Music Book, Song Book
Hymn Book, Service Book

Also available from us courtesy of Oxford University Press:
Young Readers' Dictionary
(large print edition)
Young Readers' Thesaurus
(large print edition)

For further information or a free brochure, please contact us at:
Ulverscroft Large Print Books Ltd.,
The Green, Bradgate Road, Anstey,
Leicester, LE7 7FU, England.
Tel: (00 44) 0116 236 4325
Fax: (00 44) 0116 234 0205